Eric jumped down from the wagon and hurried to the other side, where he helped Michaela down.

As her foot hit the ground, she lost her balance and fell against Eric's chest. She looked up into his eyes, and before she knew what was happening, his lips met hers.

For a moment, she felt herself responding.

"No!" She pushed herself away, still feeling the burning sensation on her lips.

"I'm sorry." Eric looked down at her. "I didn't plan to kiss you, Michaela. It just seemed so natural."

"It's not that; it's just. . ."

Questions flashed through her mind as she tried to stop the panic rising in her throat. What about Philip? She started to slowly back away from Eric.

"Wait, Michaela." Eric gently brushed a snowflake off the end of her nose. "Tell me the truth, Michaela. Is it just me, or do you feel something as well?"

Michaela took a deep breath, trying desperately to make sense out of her jumbled emotions. She knew she felt a strong physical attraction to Eric, but was there something more? Something deeper?

No! I'm going home to Philip.

D0591652

LISA HARRIS is a wife, mother, and author. She and her husband, Scott, along with their three children, live outside Johannesburg, South Africa, as missionaries. After graduating from Harding University with degrees in Bible and Family and Consumer Sciences, Lisa spent several years living in Europe and West Africa with her husband as church-planting missionaries. They have traveled to more than twenty countries, including France, Kenya, Japan, and Zimbabwe. Lisa has had over fifty articles, short stories, and devotionals published as well as two novellas.

Michaela's Choice

Lisa Harris

Heartsong Presents

To my son, Gabriel. I thank God for you daily and the blessing you are to our family. May you always find refuge in Him.

A note from the Author:
I love to hear from my readers! You may correspond with me by writing:

Lisa Harris
Author Relations
PO Box 719
Uhrichsville, OH 44683

ISBN 1-59310-429-4

MICHAELA'S CHOICE

Our mission is to publish and distribute inspirational products offering exceptional value and biblical encouragement to the masses.

All Scripture quotations are taken from the King James Version of the Bible.

All of the characters and events in this book are fictitious. Any resemblance to actual persons, living or dead, or to actual events is purely coincidental.

PRINTED IN THE U.S.A.

Or check out our Web site at www.heartsongpresents.com

prologue

Outskirts of Boston, winter 1881

Michaela Macintosh woke to her own screams. The terror of that night had returned, bathing her in a pool of sweat. It was the same dream she'd had since the night of the fire. The house appeared, and she found herself standing in Leah's bedroom with flames licking at her flesh. In slow motion, Michaela tried desperately to reach out through the horror surrounding her to find her husband and daughter. The muddled screams had grown louder until she finally awoke, realizing the frantic cries were her own.

The door to her room opened, and by the pale light of the moon, she watched as Aunt Clara slipped in and sat on the bed beside her shivering form.

"It's all right." Aunt Clara put her arms around Michaela and held her tight. "It was only another nightmare."

Michaela tried unsuccessfully to control the sobs that came and finally gave in, crying until there weren't any tears left. There had been fewer nightmares in the last six months, but when the dream did come, it brought with it the stark reality of that night. Longing to push the lingering images away from her, she forced herself to take slow, deep breaths. But unanswered questions continued to haunt her.

After several minutes, the intense feelings of panic left, only to be replaced with a deep void. "Why did Ethen and

Leah have to die? I miss them so much."

Aunt Clara stroked her hair, gently pushing the damp strands away from Michaela's face. "I wish I could take your pain away. All I know is that God has promised to go through the valleys with us, and He will carry us through times of trouble. 'The LORD redeemeth the soul of his servants: and none of them that trust in him shall be desolate.'"

Listening to the words her aunt recited from Psalm 34, Michaela knew that God had compassion for her. Yet at the moment, He seemed so far away.

"Do you want me to stay until you fall asleep?" Aunt Clara asked.

Michaela nodded and closed her eyes, emotionally exhausted from the ordeal. *When will You take away the pain, Lord?*

Aunt Clara's strong alto voice broke through the quiet of the night. "'What a friend we have in Jesus, all our sins and grief to bear. What a privilege to carry, everything to God in prayer.'"

The words from the hymn worked as a salve on Michaela's spirit, and before long, she drifted off into a dreamless slumber.

one

Six months later

Michaela looked out her second-story bedroom window toward the ocean. A ship followed the breeze into the harbor, its majestic white sails billowing in the wind. What would it be like to sail on a vessel that could take her to another place? Another time? Another life?

That's what she wanted now—to get away. Far away where she could forget. But she knew she would never be able to. How could she erase the moment her life changed forever? How could she get over losing a spouse and a child? It had taken only an instant for the fire to snatch their lives away— an instant to tear her entire life apart. All she could do now was try in vain to push back the memories that constantly invaded her thoughts.

Michaela opened the door of the mahogany wardrobe that sat in the corner of her room. Ethen's skilled hands had created the masterpiece with its ornate front panels and twisted barley crown. When he and his brother, Philip, had taken over their father's cabinetmaking business ten years ago, they'd found success in what they did.

Ethen had been the dreamer and early on had shown an incredible talent to see beyond a raw piece of wood to the finished product. Philip also was gifted in woodwork, but he excelled on the business side and had the ability to take

Ethen's artistic flair and turn it into a thriving business. Now Philip was the only one left to keep the family business going.

Michaela pulled a dress from the inside of the armoire inlaid with cedar and breathed in the fragrant scent of the wood. Of all the dresses she owned, this had been Ethen's favorite. How many times had he told her that the tiny green-flowered print brought out the red in her hair and accented her fair skin?

Today she wore it because the collar, trimmed with antique lace, was high enough to hide the scars that still covered her neck and left shoulder. Pausing to look at her reflection in the beveled mirror beside the wardrobe, she ran her fingers across the scars to where they stopped at the base of her neck. The doctor told her that with time the disfigurement would fade, but the raised welts were still noticeable.

Why was it that everything seemed to point back to that night a year and a half ago, reminding her of what she had lost? Turning away from the mirror, she dressed quickly, then pinned the small watch that had been her mother's onto the dress's bodice. She had thirty minutes until her first student arrived. Aunt Clara had been right. Teaching piano lessons gave her a way to occupy her time and stay busy.

Normally she enjoyed the time interacting with her students, but at the moment, music was the last thing on her mind. Today the committee would decide Anna's future and whether or not they would allow Michaela to raise her. Five-year-old Anna, with her bright smile and angelic face, had lost her parents in the same fire that had taken Ethen and Leah. She'd become the one constant source of joy in Michaela's life.

Hurrying down the narrow staircase that led to the parlor below, she prayed fervently that God would answer her prayer that the board would grant her custody of Anna.

The curtains of the small parlor were open, letting the morning sun spill across the rose-colored walls. She loved this old house. It was the home she'd come to after her parents were killed in a buggy accident when she was only fourteen years old. And the home she'd come back to after Ethen and Leah died.

She ran her hand across a brightly flowered slipcover her best friend, Caroline, had made last winter for Aunt Clara's sofa. As a child, Michaela had called this the happy room because it reminded her of family and love. Countless Christmases had been spent here in front of the stone fireplace, singing carols and drinking hot chocolate or celebrating a birthday with presents. She had never lacked for anything—especially love.

Pushing memories of the past aside, Michaela stepped into the kitchen. The sunny yellow room heralded a nice-sized window overlooking her aunt's garden, exquisite no matter what time of the year with its array of flowers and assorted shades of greenery.

Aunt Clara stood in front of the cast-iron stove, wearing the familiar white apron over her dress while frying a pan of eggs and potatoes. Her brother-in-law sat at the table.

"What brings you by so early, Philip?" Michaela greeted her aunt with a kiss on her cheek, then turned to her late husband's younger brother.

"Your aunt's dresser's almost ready." Philip raked his fingertips through his dark, curly hair and leaned back in his chair. "I had a question to ask her about the mirror we're getting ready to mount."

"Truth is, he just wanted a homemade meal." Aunt Clara

put her hands on her hips. "How can a man expect to work as hard as you do with no one to fix you a proper meal every day?" She took a step toward him and offered a smile. "Marietta told me that Molly Granger's back in town. She's a beautiful girl—"

"I manage just fine, Aunt Clara." Philip laughed, then took a bite of his eggs. "I haven't gone hungry yet."

In spite of her somber mood, Michaela smiled at her aunt's matchmaking attempts. Finding a wife for Philip had become one of Aunt Clara's ambitions. Barely a Sunday went by that she didn't invite at least one single woman over for dinner if Philip was able to join them. After last week's disastrous meal with Julia Hurst, Michaela was certain it would be weeks before Philip returned for another Sunday meal. The woman had talked nonstop for two hours, sharing anecdotes about the pet Pekingese her father had given her for her birthday. Even Michaela had longed to slip out of the room during the tedious monologue.

"One of these days you'll meet the woman you've been waiting for, and you'll thank me." Aunt Clara clicked her tongue and began dishing up another plate. "This is for you, Michaela. You need to eat, too."

Michaela raised her hand in protest. "I don't think I want anything this morning. Maybe just a glass of orange juice."

"Nonsense. You have to eat." Aunt Clara finished piling the food on the plate and set it on the table.

Michaela poured a glass of juice from the pitcher, trying to ignore the growing ache in her temple.

"You need to go down to the shop and see the dresser, Michaela," Aunt Clara said. "The detail in the woodwork is exquisite. I don't know how you do it, Philip."

"I'm glad you like it. Truthfully, though, the dresser's not the only reason I came by this morning." Philip's cheerful expression turned serious. "The committee's making their decision about Anna today, aren't they?"

"Yes." Michaela sat down, and the pounding in her forehead intensified. "I'm spending the afternoon at the orphanage. Caroline's in charge of today's fund-raiser, and I told her I'd help out. I should have their decision by the time it's over."

"How are you feeling?" Worry lines creased Aunt Clara's forehead.

"Scared. . .anxious. . .worried." Michaela spread a spoonful of homemade cranberry and apple jam on a biscuit and took a tasteless bite. "I'm trying not to think about it, but I don't ever remember being as nervous as I am right now."

"I saw Agnes in town yesterday." Aunt Clara pulled out one of the wooden chairs from the table and sat beside her. "She sounded optimistic that things would work out for you and Anna."

Michaela fiddled with the white linen napkin in her lap and shook her head. "If it were up to Agnes, Anna would be mine, but unfortunately, the decision's not hers to make."

"The people in this town respect you," Philip said as he added a spoonful of sugar to his coffee and slowly stirred it. "They know what a wonderful Christian woman you are and that all you want is what's best for Anna."

"But am I doing what's best for her?" Michaela clenched her hands into fists in her lap. "I've prayed so hard, but sometimes I'm just not sure. Part of me understands their hesitation in letting a child be adopted into a home where there isn't a father, but Anna's like a daughter to me. She was Leah's best friend ever since they could toddle around together, and she practically lived at our house."

How many times had she sat in the parlor with Anna and Leah in their dress-up clothes, surrounded by dolls and tea-cups? They'd spent countless hours baking gingerbread cookies in the kitchen and swinging from the big oak tree in their backyard. The realization that she'd never have another sunny afternoon with Leah hurt so badly at times, she could hardly take another breath.

"Does the pain ever go away?" She rested her forehead against her fingertips for a moment, trying to hold back a flood of tears that threatened to overflow.

"No, not entirely." Aunt Clara shook her head slowly. "It's been almost ten years since I lost my Henry, and I still miss him. The pain eases, slowly at times, but it will ease."

Michaela took a deep breath, then let it out slowly. "I feel so lost. I don't know what direction my life is headed. It used to be enough to be a mother and a wife, but now that's gone. It's almost as though in losing my family, I lost my identity, and now I don't even know if they'll let me be a mother again."

Aunt Clara caught Michaela's solemn gaze. "Keep praying and looking to the Lord for direction. He'll show you the way. You're young and have many options open before you."

Philip reached out and squeezed Michaela's hand. "I need to get back to the store, but promise me you'll stop by on the way home if you find out anything."

Michaela nodded and stood up. "I'll walk you outside."

"Thank you for breakfast." Philip kissed Aunt Clara on the cheek and followed Michaela out the front door.

Resting her hand in the crook of Philip's arm, Michaela accompanied him slowly down the brick walk toward the street. The sun filtered through the trees, warming her face but failing to reach the depths of her heart.

"Do you have any lessons this morning?" he asked.

"Four, including Sammy."

Philip let out a deep chuckle. "Sammy Hauk?"

"The one and only."

"Sammy's name invokes visions of last summer's disastrous church picnic when he let a snake loose in the middle of Mrs. Lindberg's prized cakes."

Michaela felt the corners of her mouth curl into a smile at the memory. "He's a character."

"You're working too hard, Michaela." Philip stopped at the front gate and turned to face her. "I worry about you."

"Staying busy is good for me."

"Not if you run yourself ragged. You need more rest. Time to do something just for yourself."

"You're beginning to sound like Aunt Clara." Michaela squeezed his hand. "I enjoy what I do."

"And you're very good at it. But I do worry about you."

"Don't. I'm fine. And after today, if the committee will let me adopt Anna. . ." She let her voice trail off, afraid to envision the two of them together as a family. Afraid of the pain that would come if the board said no.

Leaning against the fence, Michaela tried to push aside the discouraging thoughts. "Caroline talked me into bringing two cakes to the bake sale today. We should raise enough money to be able to buy each of the children the coats, sweaters, and shoes they will need this winter, as well as supplies for school. And did you hear the news that Samuel Perkins is donating ten new beds for the children? Anna told me—"

He tilted her chin with his index finger and smiled. "You're rambling."

She chewed on the inside of her lip. "I ramble when I'm nervous."

Grasping both her hands, he held them tight. "I know this is hard, but I'll always be here for you. I never told you this, but when you and Ethen first got married, he made me promise that if anything ever happened to him, I'd take care of you."

Michaela reached up and wiped away a stray tear from her cheek. "He loved you so much. You were more than just a brother. You were his best friend, and he trusted you completely."

"I take my promises very seriously. If there's anything you need, anything at all. . ."

He gathered her into his arms, and for a brief moment, everything in her world felt right again.

&

Her last lesson over, Michaela glanced at her watch, pleased to find that she still had plenty of time to eat lunch with her aunt before leaving for the orphanage. Not finding Aunt Clara in the kitchen, she wasn't surprised to see her working in one of the flowerbeds behind the house.

"I don't know how you do it." Michaela walked past a grouping of plants her aunt had arranged on a small, rustic table and stepped onto the velvety grass. "You truly are an artist."

A slightly terraced lawn surrounded the fishpond Michaela's uncle had put in shortly before he died. Solid oak trees stood valiantly around the yard, shading the ground from the harsh summer sun. But the most treasured place was where Aunt Clara had planted her prize garden of roses, columbine, rhododendron, and cardinal flowers.

"There are many different kinds of artists," her aunt said

with a smile. "You're an artist with your music."

Michaela stopped where Aunt Clara worked and sat down on the grass beside her. "You can smell the saltwater in the air today." She breathed in deeply, attempting to allow the familiar scent to soothe her spirit.

Clara eased herself up to a standing position. "I plan to go by the store this afternoon. Do you need anything?"

"I don't think so." Michaela plucked a blade of grass and twirled it between her fingers. What she needed couldn't be bought at a store or found at any seller's stand. Anna was an intricate part of her life. One she couldn't bear to lose.

Clara's concern showed in her eyes as she spoke. "Still thinking about the committee's decision?"

Michaela stood and followed her aunt into the house. "I'll know soon enough, so there's no use fretting about it."

Clara turned around to face her niece. "Somehow, I have the feeling the board's going to grant your request."

"I hope you're right," Michaela whispered. "I hope you're right."

two

Michaela walked the short distance to the Mills Street Orphanage, praying the entire way. From her vantage point, it was going to take a miracle for the committee to allow her to keep Anna, so she was praying for a miracle. Tightening her grip on the box that held the two cakes she'd baked the day before, she slowly made her way up the walk toward the Romanesque-style home where Anna lived.

"Looks like you've been busy." Caroline Hodges greeted Michaela at the front door of the orphanage with a broad smile and peeked inside the box. "Yum. You made my favorite. Chocolate."

Michaela grinned at her friend's predictable response. "I knew if no one else bought them, you would."

Caroline reached up and brushed back a wisp of her short, curly bangs with her fingertips and laughed. "You know me far too well."

Together they entered the familiar parlor of the large house where Michaela had spent numerous afternoons visiting with Anna. The furniture, a collection of hand-me-down items from a circular sofa to several Chippendale chairs, had been rearranged to make room for the assortment of desserts that would be sold during the fund-raiser.

"This is going to be quite an afternoon." Caroline smoothed down the front of her blue taffeta skirt, then busied herself in arranging the table. "We've just opened for business and already sold three cakes and two pies."

Michaela eyed the heavy pine table already laden with a variety of homemade pies, cakes, and colorfully wrapped boxes of peanut brittle, taffy, and other candies.

Noting a box filled with pralines, Michaela resisted a second look. "I can tell you right now, I'm going to have to stay out of this room. If they taste as good as they smell. . ."

Caroline moved a few of the confections and set Michaela's cakes in a prominent position on the white tablecloth. "You know yours will go for the highest price."

"Caroline." Michaela shook her head at the biased compliment and grinned. "Spoken by a devoted best friend."

"It's true. I had to promise myself I wouldn't take a single bite." Caroline giggled, fairly drooling over the rich assortment of goodies. Her love for sweets had helped contribute to her pleasant but plump figure. "If I gain another pound, I'll have to buy a whole new wardrobe."

The sound of children's laughter floated into the parlor, and Michaela glanced past Caroline into the adjoining room. "Have you seen Anna today?"

"She's wearing the sweetest pink calico dress with a matching apron. She'll be so excited to see you." Caroline turned from the table and looked at Michaela. "I almost forgot. The committee's making their decision today, aren't they?"

"Yes." Michaela's voice quivered. "Agnes is supposed to let me know their answer this afternoon."

"I know that many people are praying for you." Caroline reached out and rested her hand against Michaela's arm. "Agnes had to run out for a bit, but she'll be back soon."

Michaela turned as someone called her name. She sighed, spotting Vivian Lockhart entering the room from the other side of the house and wished there was a way to avoid the nosy woman.

"I know she's a difficult person to get along with," Caroline whispered to Michaela, "but her mother donated fifty dollars to the orphanage this morning. I'll be forever in your debt if you talk to her." Before Michaela could respond, Caroline hurried away to help an older woman who had just brought two homemade pies to sell.

Vivian looked dramatic, as usual, in a pink organdy day dress with matching pink ribbon trim. Knowing there was nowhere to hide, Michaela smiled and waited as Vivian approached.

"It seems like I haven't seen you for ages, Michaela. You look wonderful, and that dress is gorgeous."

Michaela knew her outfit could never be called stylish but thanked her for the compliment anyway, barely getting out the words before Vivian began again.

"Tell me, what have you been up to?" True to her nature, Vivian didn't wait for Michaela's answer. "I hear you're trying to adopt one of the poor orphans. I told my mother what a perfect solution for both you and the child. So sad for her to have lost both parents in that terrible fire. Of course, my mother wasn't convinced it's a good idea with your being a widow, but you know how Mother is."

Exactly like her mother, always talking without thinking first. Michaela gritted her teeth but stifled a reply when she felt someone tug on her skirt. Looking down into the eyes of a dark-haired five-year-old, all traces of frustration toward Vivian left.

"Anna!" Michaela gave the small child a big hug, her heart softening at the sight of the young girl.

"I knew you'd come today." Anna's brown eyes brightened

and lit up her entire face.

"Tell me, sweetheart, what have you been up to?" Michaela knelt down and pushed back a strand of hair from Anna's heart-shaped face, tucking it behind her ear.

"Right now we're eating lunch, and this afternoon we're going to play all kinds of games. There's even going to be prizes."

Michaela could hear the children's happy chatter as they finished lunch in the dining room. "I'm going to be here the whole afternoon."

Anna clapped her hands together and gave Michaela another hug.

Vivian had already gone to talk to a group of women who'd just entered the room, and Caroline, who was busy arranging the food table, seemed to have everything under control.

"Would you like to go for a walk before the games start?" Michaela asked.

Anna nodded, and after checking with one of the staff members, Michaela and Anna headed to their favorite spot. Several hundred feet behind the house stood a huge oak tree. It was the perfect thinking spot, Anna had told her one afternoon, and then and there, they had proclaimed it their special place. When they got to the tree, Michaela sat down next to Anna and leaned back against the thick bark.

"It's a beautiful day, isn't it, Anna?" A clear blue sky fanned out above them, dotted only by a few puffy white clouds.

"I suppose."

Michaela looked down and caught Anna's sullen expression. "What is it?"

Anna crossed her legs and fiddled with the hem of her dress. "I had another dream last night. I was looking for my mommy and daddy, but I couldn't find them."

Michaela pulled Anna into her lap and held her close. A tear trickled down the little girl's face. "I tried to save them, really I did."

"I know, sweetheart. It wasn't your fault." Michaela knew the words were true, yet she often struggled with the same feelings of guilt for not having been able to save Ethen and Leah. "Sometimes I have bad dreams, too."

"You do?" Anna's eyes narrowed at the thought.

"Sometimes I dream I'm trying to save Ethen."

"And Leah?"

"Yes. And Leah."

"Leah was my best friend."

Why did so many people have to die, Lord? My husband and my daughter? Anna's parents? How can I even begin to take away Anna's pain?

Michaela took a deep breath and searched for the right words. "Do you remember what to do when you're sad or afraid, Anna?"

"Yes." Anna snuggled closer into Michaela's arms. "I try to remember how much God loves me. And I remember that they're in heaven with Jesus, and someday I'll see them again."

"That's exactly what you need to think about."

Anna leaned her head back and looked into Michaela's eyes. "I wish you were my mother."

Michaela desperately wished the same thing. She pulled Anna tight against her and breathed in the faint scent of lavender from her hair, struggling with how much to tell Anna about her attempts to adopt her. Surely it was best for her not to know in case the committee turned her down. For now, her frequent visits would have to do.

"Why don't you tell me about your friends." She rocked Anna slowly back and forth, treasuring this time they had together. "What did you do yesterday?"

They talked until the bell rang, announcing the beginning of the activities. Michaela stood, took Anna's small hand, and led her back to the house. For the moment, unpleasant memories from the past were forgotten.

By the time the afternoon's festivities had ended, the children's faces were lit with smiles, and laughter filled the yard. When the dinner bell sounded, Michaela told Anna she needed to take care of something and went to find Agnes. The decision should have been made by now. It was time to face her future.

Let it be with Anna, Lord. Please, let it be with her.

⁊⦁

Michaela sat down in an old but comfortable chair across from a heavy pine desk. Like the entire home, Agnes's office was decorated simply. Bookshelves covered two walls, while a third showcased a large picture window that overlooked the front courtyard. Michaela studied the green lawn that was bordered with a colorful assortment of flowers as Agnes took a seat behind the desk.

"The time you spend here means so much to the children." Agnes pushed a pair of wire spectacles up the bridge of her nose and smiled. "They're always asking when you'll be back."

"They do a lot for me as well." It hadn't taken long for the weekly visits to the orphanage to become one of the highlights of Michaela's life. "At first I thought being around the children would be too painful, but instead it's helped me tremendously."

"I admire your courage." Agnes's smile faded. "I wish I could do something, but these decisions are not left up to me. I know you'd be a wonderful mother for Anna, but the committee has made their decision. I'm so sorry, Michaela. They want Anna to be adopted by a couple."

Michaela stared out the window, her stomach tightening as the reality of the decision hit her. Tears stung her eyes, and she blinked rapidly to stop the flow.

"If you were to marry again, I know the board would reconsider—"

"I can't marry for those reasons." Michaela's knuckles whitened as she gripped the sides of her chair and battled for control over her emotions. "That would be wrong."

Agnes tugged on her ruffled blouse. "You're right. I'm sorry to have even suggested it."

It wasn't fair. How could they have decided against her? Anna needed a home with someone who loved her. Why couldn't that be her? Michaela folded her hands, then pulled them apart nervously. "I'm sorry, Agnes. I know this isn't your fault; it's just that I felt so sure this was God's will for Anna and me. I love her so much, and after losing Leah, well, I thought God was giving me another daughter."

"If there's anything I can do. . ." Agnes picked up a pencil and tapped it against the desk, obviously dismayed by the outcome of the board's answer. But Agnes didn't have to live with the consequences of their decision.

"Please tell Anna and the others good-bye for me." Michaela shook her head numbly and stood. "I need to go home."

"Before you leave, there is one more thing." Agnes dropped her gaze and tapped rapidly again against the wood with the pencil. "There's a couple interested in adopting Anna."

Michaela's eyes grew wide with disbelief, and a feeling of panic swept over her. *No, Lord, please don't take her away from me so soon.*

"They've been by several times and are interested in the idea of adopting an older child, possibly even two. They want to take their time and get to know her, but they plan to make a decision soon."

Michaela bit her lip, determined to hold back the tears until she was home in the sanctuary of her room. *Don't do this to me, God. It's too much.*

"I know this coming at the same time as the committee's decision is not easy, but I felt like I needed to let you know. They're a wonderful Christian couple who have never had children and feel called by God to adopt."

"I wish more couples felt that way." Michaela's words came automatically as she battled to calm the turmoil raging inside.

"Michaela, what you do here with the children means more to them than you will ever imagine." She dropped the pencil onto the table and leaned forward in her chair. "I believe that someday God is going to bless you with more children."

Michaela looked at Agnes, a raw ache radiating through her body. "You don't know what God's going to do. God took away my husband. He took away my baby. And now He's taken away Anna. Don't try to tell me what God's going to do!"

❧

How dare they come between Anna and me.

Michaela walked along the crowded street the few blocks toward Philip's shop, her feet pounding the ground beneath her. How could the members of the committee make a decision like that? Couldn't they understand the relationship she had with Anna was as strong a bond as a mother had with her biological child? How could they just rip Anna out of her life in order to follow what seemed appropriate to society?

She'd prayed about this situation for so long and felt this was what God wanted her to do. They might not be a traditional family, but she and Anna understood each other. They loved each other. Why couldn't they see that?

The front room of the cabinetry shop was quiet when Michaela entered the building, slamming the door behind her.

"Philip?" Michaela ran her hand across an unfinished table near the back of the room. A splinter lodged in her index finger and a pool of blood rushed to the surface. She pulled out the piece of wood, easing the sting of the injury. If only the pain in her heart could fade as quickly.

"Michaela." Philip entered the room from the back, his clothes layered with a thin covering of sawdust. He ran his hand through his dark hair as if trying to smooth it out. "Did you find out anything?"

"They won't let me adopt Anna." Saying the words aloud only resulted in making them seem real.

"I'm so sorry." He bridged the gap between them and gathered her into his arms. "I know how much you love her."

"I'm so angry, all I want to do is scream." She took a step back, her voice rising with each word. Even Philip couldn't take away the hurt this time. "They met me briefly during one interview, and with that, they think they have all the information they need to decide our fate.

"What about the fact that I was at her mother's side when Anna was born? I took care of her when her parents were sick and helped to plan her birthday parties. I was the one who held Anna while she sobbed over the death of her parents."

She crossed the room, her mind numb with grief. Turning

sharply to face Philip, she slammed her palms against the top of a wooden dresser. "I don't understand, Philip. What does God want from me? Wasn't I a good enough mother for Leah? Is this His way of punishing me? I lost one child and now I'm losing Anna."

"No, Michaela, of course not!" Philip came and stood beside her. She could see the disappointment reflected in his eyes. "You were a wonderful mother to Leah. I can't tell you why this happened, but I do know that God isn't punishing you."

She wanted to believe him, but the hurt wouldn't let her.

"Is there any way to reverse their decision?" He reached out and pushed back a strand of hair that had fallen into her eyes.

She shook her head. "The decision is final, unless, of course, I get married. Then they might reconsider their decision."

"You don't have a suitor hidden anywhere, do you?"

Michaela raised her head and allowed a slight grin. Only Philip could make her smile at a time like this. "Not the last time I checked."

"Then we'll have to think of something else." He glanced at the clock that hung on the back wall. "It's almost dinnertime. Would you like to go eat? Maybe it would help get your mind off everything for a little while."

"I do believe you're always thinking about food." Michaela had been right to come. Philip was the one person who could help her get through this.

"I work up a big appetite. Just ask your aunt," he said with a lopsided grin.

Michaela looked at Philip, still in his work clothes. His hands were calloused, and his arms showed the strength of someone who was no stranger to physical labor. Looking into his familiar blue eyes, she saw her friend and confidant, and for the moment, some of the anger seemed to dissipate. "Thank you."

"For what?"

"For always being there for me. For knowing how to make me smile."

⋆

Philip looked at Michaela and felt an unexplained stir.

"What is it?" Michaela asked.

"Nothing," Philip stammered, his heart beating faster at the idea that had suddenly taken form in his mind. *Could this be the answer, God? If I marry Michaela, we could be a family. We could adopt Anna.*

Sunlight came in from the window behind Michaela, casting a golden glow around her. Her red hair shimmered in the light, and the downward tilt of her mouth almost made him want to kiss her. The thought came totally unexpectedly.

Why have I never noticed how beautiful she is, God? He knew her heart and what a caring and compassionate person she was, but could he have feelings for her? Buried feelings he never knew existed?

They'd become close after Ethen's and Leah's deaths. Michaela had turned to him for the comfort and support she needed, and he had never felt as at ease around a woman as he did with Michaela. He'd always seen Michaela as a sister and a good friend, but now he found himself looking at her as more than his brother's widow. Was there a chance their relationship could develop into something deeper?

"I heard the new restaurant in town has wonderful fish chowder."

At Michaela's suggestion, he pushed his thoughts aside for

the moment—until he could deal with them in the silence of his room above the shop. "We could invite your aunt."

"I'd like that." Michaela wiped the back of her hand across her tear-stained face and smiled.

"Let me go get out of my work clothes, then I'll bring the buggy around and meet you out front. I was planning to close up in a few minutes, anyway."

Philip hurried to change out of his work clothes, praying for wisdom the entire way. Something told him, as he went out the back and locked the door behind him, that his entire life was about to change.

&

"Have a good time tonight," Aunt Clara said as Philip and Michaela walked toward the front of the house.

"Are you sure you don't want to go?" Michaela lingered in the open doorway.

"Positive." Aunt Clara smiled and ran her hand down Michaela's cheek, then turned to Philip. "Thank you for getting her out of the house and helping get her mind off of today. If I hadn't worn myself out in the garden, I might have come, but I'd planned a leisurely evening with a good book I borrowed from Amy Parker, and that's exactly what I'm going to do."

"If you're sure. . ."

"Go on," she exclaimed, hurrying them out the door.

Philip helped Michaela into the buggy, then climbed in beside her. Her satin dress, the color of emeralds, shimmered in the fading sunlight. Her beauty, though familiar, amazed him. It was as if he were seeing her for the first time.

"You're quiet tonight," Michaela said a few minutes after they left the house.

"Just concerned about you." Philip kept his eyes on the road, afraid of his growing feelings toward the woman who sat beside him. "I know you've spent a lot of time in prayer over Anna's adoption, and I've also been praying they'd say yes."

"I want what's best for her, but I can't help believing that what's best for her is me."

For the past hour, Philip hadn't been able to dismiss the idea of asking her to marry him. The thought of them together seemed so right. Philip loved Anna, and the three of them had spent countless afternoons together in the past year. They could be a family.

As he allowed himself to steal a glance at Michaela, everything seemed clear. He would ask Michaela to marry him, and they would adopt Anna. Maybe it wasn't love yet, but one thing was for sure: Michaela held a piece of his heart, and he wasn't about to take it back.

three

Michaela felt a ribbon of peace encircle her as she walked beside Philip along one of the streets that overlooked the incoming swells of the ocean. She'd enjoyed the well-prepared dinner of corned beef and potatoes, but more than anything else, she'd enjoyed spending the evening with Philip.

There were very few people who understood her the way he did. She had vented and poured out her frustrations, and the entire time he'd listened, never once trying to fix everything or judge her heated reaction toward the board's decision. Instead, he grieved with her, cried with her, and prayed with her.

"Are you all right?" Philip placed her hand in the crook of his arm.

"I think so." The pain lingered, but some of the sting had lessened. "Today was heartbreaking, but I realize that staying angry won't change the situation."

Michaela glanced at Philip. He always knew how to make her laugh and knew exactly what to say to lift her spirits. As the shadows of twilight moved across the waters, she studied the silhouette of his tall figure. Every movement he made with his broad shoulders and long legs demonstrated strength.

She stopped to hold on to a railing so she could gaze out across the constant flow of the tide. "It's beautiful out tonight, isn't it?"

The last of the fading sunlight glistened off the dark waves, and she didn't think there could be another place as peaceful as this.

"It's getting late." She caught the longing in Philip's voice as he spoke and wondered if he wanted to prolong the evening as much as she did. "I guess I'd better take you home now."

∂

Philip remained silent, lost in thought, as he walked Michaela to the door of Aunt Clara's house. He wondered what it would be like to kiss her.

"Michaela," he began as they reached the door.

"Yes?"

In the silver light of the moon, he could see her face and hear her breathing. He had to slow down. He had to wait until he could sort out the myriad of emotions he felt.

"I'll see you in a few days," he said. "I have to go out of town tomorrow to deliver an order."

"You don't normally make deliveries, do you?" Her eyes widened, but he couldn't read her expression. Did she care that he would be gone for a while?

"A couple of workers are out this week, and it has to be done. I'll be back on Friday." A torrent of emotions erupted as she touched his arm with the tips of her fingers.

"Be careful, and thank you for this evening. In spite of all that happened today, I needed this."

"Me, too." He resisted his desire to run his thumb down her cheek, wishing he had the words to take away the pain he knew she felt.

"I almost forgot; Aunt Clara wanted me to invite you over for dinner Friday evening. Will you be back in time?"

He nodded and felt a rush of anticipation. "I won't be back too late."

"Wonderful. We'll eat at seven."

"Perfect." If only he didn't have to wait until Friday to see her again.

ॐ

He was in love with his brother's wife.

An hour later, Philip stood in the middle of his workroom, rubbing oil into the Queen Anne desk he'd finished earlier that afternoon. Did the fact that Ethen was dead really make a difference? What would Ethen think if he knew that the feelings he felt for Michaela had crossed beyond innocent friendship to wanting to ask her to spend the rest of her life with him?

Ethen is dead!

Philip poured more oil on the cloth, then pressed it harder against the rich copper-colored grain. He felt at home with a piece of wood in his hands. The process of taking the raw material and forming it into something useful was a progression of change and development. Just like his relationship with Michaela.

For years, Michaela had been Ethen's wife. As a man, Philip had appreciated her beauty and sweet temperament, but his feelings had never gone beyond what was appropriate. She was a friend and close family member. Nothing more. Even after Ethen's death, he'd never imagined feeling the way he did tonight. But now that line had been crossed.

Never again could he watch her smile without his heart pounding in his chest or feel her soft hand against his arm without longing to engulf it in his own. No. Things could never be the same again.

He'd listened to her tonight as she'd poured out her frustrations over losing Anna, and his heart broke with hers. His feelings of loss over Anna's adoption couldn't compare to hers, but he still experienced grief and heartache because she felt those things.

Wait on the Lord: be of good courage, and he shall strengthen thine heart: wait, I say, on the Lord. The verse from Psalm 27 came to mind as Philip moved to the other side of the desk and continued to vigorously polish the wood. For years he had waited for the one whom God would choose for him to share his life with. The one he would someday call his wife. Was Michaela the reason he had never given his heart to anyone else?

Other questions haunted him. Could he share his feelings with Michaela? And if he did, would she understand? Was it even a possibility that she might come to feel the way he did? He threw the rag against the wood and let out a deep sigh. Resting his hands against the decorative panel, he shook his head. He couldn't get over the feeling he was betraying his brother's trust. But Ethen was dead. Ethen would want Michaela to find happiness with someone else. Why not with him?

❧

As soon as Michaela finished her last piano lesson the next day, she made her way to the garden behind the house. In spite of the late summer heat, her aunt had managed to keep the flowers and plants thriving.

"Looks like we'll have plenty of fresh vegetables this fall." Michaela greeted Aunt Clara with a smile. Night had brought with it an array of uncertainties and fears, but in the light of day, she'd managed to keep her emotions under control.

"I might have gone a bit overboard." Aunt Clara glanced up from a healthy tomato plant. "I don't know why, but I went ahead and planted twice what I normally do."

"We both enjoy it, and no one complains when you give the extra away." Michaela sat down in the warm grass and stretched her legs out in front of her.

"I guess you're right." Aunt Clara went back to tending to her plants like a mother doting on her young. "There's a letter from Daniel for you on the porch rail."

"I must have missed it when I came out." Michaela stood and walked back toward the porch, eager to read the news from her brother. "Did I tell you Philip will be coming over for dinner tomorrow night?"

"Good. I thought I'd make some of my mother's Irish stew."

Michaela picked up the envelope and tapped the edge against her palm. "Philip certainly won't complain."

"That boy could use some home cooking, though what he really needs is a good woman."

"You know I've tried to introduce him to some of the women at church, but he always says they're too old, or too young, or they talk too much." Michaela slipped the thin paper from the envelope. "I've decided to stay out of it from now on. Seems to just get me into trouble."

Michaela took the letter over to a small wrought iron bench on the other side of her aunt and sat down. "I still can't believe it's been six years since Daniel and Emma left Boston."

Michaela looked down at the wrinkled paper and began to read aloud.

Dear Aunt Clara and Michaela,

It's well into summer here, and every year I seem to enjoy living in this area more. I wish you could see this beautiful part of Massachusetts someday. Cranton is only a short distance from the Connecticut River, and we are surrounded by forests of pines that blend into the farms and orchards around us. This is a place that grows on you, and I can't imagine living anywhere else.

We have some good news to tell you. Emma is expecting again. I guess the news comes with mixed emotions and concerns since we have already lost two children.

The doctor is worried, but he told us if she can carry the baby past the next two months, she has a good chance of delivering a healthy baby in late December. Please remember to lift us up to the Father in your prayers. Emma is strong, but the last two years have been very difficult. Losing two babies has been hard on her, both physically and emotionally, yet she amazes me with her strength and faith in God.

Things on the farm are going well. The crops have been very good this year. We also have several prize pigs we will butcher this fall. Our apple trees are thriving, and we have a growing number of cattle and horses. I thank God every day for the land and what it gives us. I have come a long way from a newly married youngster who many said had a foolish dream of becoming a farmer.

Our closest neighbor, Eric Johnson, has a farm about twice the size of ours. I think I've mentioned him to you in previous letters. He's a widower with six children whose wife died soon after we arrived. Yet he's helped us so much since our arrival in Cranton.

Yesterday one of his boys came over with a big pot of stew when they heard Emma was feeling poorly. Eric's going with me to Springfield when I sell two of my horses to help ensure I get a good price for them. I guess he has lived out here close to eighteen years now. His kids truly are a blessing, as they work hard alongside him to keep the farm going.

We're planning a fall celebration for the church and the community next month. Something we really look forward to each year. We may not have all the conveniences and luxuries found in Boston, but we will have the best supper you could imagine, with smoked beef, chicken, steak, and all the trimmings.

Michaela, we want you to know we're keeping you in our daily prayers. May God continue to heal your heart.

All our love,
Daniel and Emma

"I wish I could go see them and help Emma." Michaela set the letter down beside her and lifted up a silent prayer for Emma's pregnancy. It had been a bitter loss for the entire family when Emma miscarried during her first pregnancy, then again a year later.

"Why don't you go?" Aunt Clara looked up from the plant she was trimming.

"I couldn't leave you here alone." Michaela got up from the bench and began weeding around a bed of pink roses.

"Why not? It would be good for you to go away for a while and get some rest. The timing's perfect." She rested her hands on her hips. "I don't know why I didn't think of it earlier. Might help you get your mind off Anna, and besides, you've been working too hard lately."

"I wouldn't exactly have nothing to do if I went. I would have to help run a farm or at least do the cooking and cleaning. What do I know about farm work?"

"Michaela." Aunt Clara's glance held a measure of determination. "Maybe going to see your brother is just what you need. It would give you a chance to step back from things and figure out what direction you need to take with your life."

Michaela pulled out another weed. *Is this Your will for me, Lord?* From somewhere deep inside her, she knew her aunt was right. There were so many feelings and emotions she had buried deep within her, and just like this garden needed to be weeded and taken care of, the day would come when she would have to finish dealing with the pain from her past. If she didn't, she would never be able to go on with her life. She also knew herself well enough to know that if she took the time to think about going, she would never leave.

"I'll send a telegram tomorrow." Michaela stood and headed back into the house. A small measure of peace began to grow, giving her the confirmation she needed.

"If you like, I can send it for you," Aunt Clara said. "I need to go out this afternoon."

Michaela turned to her aunt and smiled. "I think someone's afraid I might back out."

"Not at all."

"Well then, it looks like I'm going to Cranton."

❧

On Friday, Michaela went to the orphanage with mixed emotions. She would be leaving on the train for her brother's farm in a week, and while she felt the excitement of her upcoming trip, part of her wanted to stay close to the familiar. Her aunt was right. Time away was exactly what she needed. It would give her the chance to think and see things more clearly.

Still, her stomach tightened as she thought of how Anna might react to her going away for a while. Michaela waited until after music class when the kids were playing outside and she could talk to Anna alone.

"Miss Agnes said I might have a new mommy and daddy," Anna said after sipping some tea from a small cup and saucer Michaela had given her the previous Christmas. They sat in the front parlor at a small table with four chairs: one for Michaela, one for Anna, and the other two for Anna's stuffed bears, Oliver and Sam, who had joined them for the tea party.

"Have you met them?" Michaela asked, pouring another cup of tea for Anna. She attempted to ignore the sharp sting of pain at the thought of someone else raising the little girl.

"She has long dark hair, and he has a funny mustache." Anna's face turned somber, and the corners of her mouth curved into a frown. "I don't want them for my mommy and daddy. I want you."

Michaela took a deep breath and reached over to grasp Anna's hand. "Wouldn't it be nice to have a mommy and a daddy?"

"I'm not sure." Anna scrunched up her nose. "They're going to visit me again. I heard them tell Miss Agnes they would like a girl and a boy. Maybe Johnny Philips. Does that mean he would be my brother?"

"I suppose it would. Would you like a brother?"

Anna just shrugged. "I told Miss Agnes I wanted you to be my mommy. She said you wanted to be my mommy, but you couldn't right now. Why?"

Michaela took a deep breath, trying to explain the situation as simply as she could. "You know I would like to be your mother, but some people who care about you decided it would be better for you to have both a mommy and a daddy."

"Oh." Anna did not sound convinced. "Will I still get to see you?"

"I'm sure we can work it out. No matter what happens, you'll always be very special to me."

Michaela knew she needed to talk to Anna about her upcoming trip but ached with the knowledge they would be apart. "I need to tell you about something. My brother and his wife, Emma, are going to have a baby, but she's sick. I told them I wanted to stay with them for a while to help Emma with the cooking and cleaning."

Anna sat still for a moment. "So you have to go away?"

"Yes, they live in Cranton, near the Connecticut River. Do you know where that is?"

Anna shook her head.

"I have to take a train to get there." Michaela tried to make it sound like an adventure.

"I took a train to New York once."

"I remember." Michaela smiled, trying to ignore the ache in her heart.

"When will you be back?"

"Sometime after Christmas."

Anna cocked her head. "Will you come and see me when you get back?"

"Of course I will." Michaela ruffled the little girl's hair, then tilted up her chin with her finger. "I wouldn't miss that for the world."

"Maybe I'll be living with my new mommy and daddy by then." Anna picked up Oliver and wrapped her short arms around him.

Michaela motioned for Anna and Oliver to come sit in her lap. Pulling them close, she stroked the young girl's hair and prayed for a miracle.

four

Philip made his fifth inspection in the mirror of the apartment above the store. His thick black hair lay in neat curls, and the dark blue suit that had been recently cleaned and pressed matched the color of his eyes. He straightened his collar and tried to relax.

Funny, though twenty-nine years old, he suddenly felt like a teenager again, asking Mary Lou to the social at church. But that had been fifteen years ago, and he wasn't interested in Mary Lou with her freckles and pigtails anymore. Today, he only had eyes for Michaela.

He hadn't slept for two nights, praying and wrestling with thoughts he hadn't known existed until a few days ago. He knew he couldn't wait any longer. In spite of the apprehension he felt over his newfound feelings toward Michaela, God had granted him peace. Tonight he would tell her how he felt.

His hands shook as he picked up his hat and slowly walked out the front door and down the busy sidewalk that would take him the short distance to Michaela's home. He had no idea how Michaela felt, but realizing he cared for her, he also knew he wanted to spend the rest of his life with her. He hadn't known how long these feelings had lain dormant in his heart, but he could never keep them from her, no matter what her response would be.

What had changed? Philip still wasn't sure, but it seemed

natural for them to be together. He wanted to spend the rest of his life making her happy, not because he felt sorry for her, but because he loved her.

The sun beat down on the dusty street, and Philip wasn't sure if he was perspiring because of the heat or because of his nerves. He'd never thought twice about eating dinner with Aunt Clara and Michaela. In fact, it was something he did at least once a week, usually on Sundays. Aunt Clara was constantly reminding him that he needed more home-cooked meals instead of the fare he typically bought from one of the street vendors. After tonight, though, he knew things would never be the same.

Ten minutes later, he stopped and stood at the gate of Aunt Clara's two-story home, fiddling with the paper wrapped around the small bouquet of flowers he'd brought for Michaela. The Victorian home stood on a street among other similar houses with their corbelled brick exteriors, round-arched windows, and decorative features. He had saved enough money in the past few years to build a house for the two of them near the sea, if that was what Michaela wanted.

"Philip?" Michaela poked her head out the front door.

"Michaela. . .hello. . . How are you?" He fumbled through the gate toward the porch where she stood. She looked beautiful in her plum-colored dress with its high collar.

He offered her the flowers. "You look lovely tonight."

"You're always so thoughtful." She brought the flowers close to her face and took in a deep breath. "Roses are my very favorite."

Nervously, he followed her into the house. She turned and smiled at him, leaving his heart racing in anticipation.

"Did you have a good trip, Philip?"

"It was fine. Very uneventful."

"Sit down, if you'd like." Michaela pointed to the rosewood armchair in the corner of the room.

It was the one he always sat on, but the familiarity of the situation did little to alleviate his anxiety.

"Dinner's almost ready. Aunt Clara went out to the garden to get some lettuce."

"Something smells delicious." Philip wiped his hands against his pant legs and took a deep breath before sitting in the cushioned chair.

"Aunt Clara made Irish stew for dinner." Michaela rested her hands on her hips and turned to him before leaving the room. "Would you like something to drink? I made lemonade this afternoon."

"That would be nice. Thank you."

He watched her flutter out of the room like a springtime butterfly. *Let her feel the same way I do, Lord.*

A minute later, Michaela came back into the room with two glasses of lemonade. "I have something I need to talk to you about," she said, handing him one of the tumblers. "But I want to wait until after dinner. We can sit out on the swing later, if you'd like. It's such a beautiful evening."

"Sounds perfect." He took a long sip of the sugary drink and attempted to relax. "I'd like to talk to you about something then as well."

"Of course." Michaela raised her eyebrows in question. "Are you sure you're all right? You seem. . .I don't know, nervous."

"I'm fine." For the first time in their relationship, he had nothing to say to her. He could talk about the large furniture order he received today from a wealthy couple living outside of Boston or the fact that the wife of one of his employees had just given birth to her eighth child, but he wasn't in the mood for small talk.

Aunt Clara entered the room, and Philip jumped out of his chair to greet her, thankful for the reprieve. "You look lovely this evening," he exclaimed. "Michaela told me you made some of your famous stew."

"My mother's recipe." Clara smoothed her white apron and beamed at the compliment. "Straight from Ireland."

"Shall I finish making the salad, Aunt Clara?" Michaela asked.

Clara nodded in agreement. "And as soon as that's done, we can eat."

≈

"The weather's perfect tonight." Michaela looked up at the stars that seemed to hover above them like thousands of tiny white diamonds. After a feast of stew and homemade bread, the wooden swing in the backyard was a perfect place to relax and enjoy the soft breeze that filtered in from the ocean.

"What did you need to talk to me about?" Michaela shifted in her seat so she could see his face better.

The light of the gas lamp revealed a guarded expression on Philip's face. Something was different tonight. He'd acted strangely all evening, and she couldn't imagine what he had to tell her.

Unless. . .he'd met someone.

She smiled at the idea. That must be it. She watched with interest as Philip looked down at the ground, rubbed his hands together, and shifted his weight in the swing, causing it to rock sideways.

"What is it?" Michaela pressured him with a laugh. "If

I didn't know better, I'd say you look like a lovesick puppy."

Philip squirmed again, and the swing banged gently against the wooden post, but he still didn't speak.

"That's it!" Michaela's eyes widened in excitement. She was right. He'd found someone.

"Who is it? Do you want me to guess?" Michaela started making a mental list, wondering if it was someone she knew. Vivian was far too outspoken for Philip, but she had seen him talking to Elizabeth at church several times. Or maybe it was Hannah. She was a widow with two small girls, but Philip had always said how much he loved children. Then there was always her best friend, Caroline—

"You're right, I think I've found someone." Philip raised his gaze to meet hers, and a solemn shadow crossed his face. "The problem is, she doesn't know. I'm close to this person, but I don't know how to tell her what I'm feeling."

Michaela reached out and rested her hand on his arm. "Philip, you have nothing to worry about. You're extremely handsome and a faithful Christian. You're talented and own a successful business, you're kind and generous—I could go on. What else could a woman want?"

He pulled his arm away but held her gaze. "So you think I should tell her how I feel?"

"Definitely." Excited about the possibility that Philip had found someone, her matchmaking skills began to work. "Wait a minute, what about the church social that's coming up? You could invite her, then slip away for a short walk after lunch and tell her how you feel. That would be perfect." She stood and continued mulling over the possibilities. "You need to wear the suit you're wearing tonight—"

"It's you, Michaela."

"And don't forget to bring her flowers. Women love flowers. . . ."

"Michaela, I said it's you."

Michaela sat back down on the swing and looked him straight in the eye. "What did you say?"

"I—I just didn't know how to tell you," Philip stammered. "I'm in love with you, Michaela."

"I don't know what to say." She was shocked at his declaration of love. Michaela had certainly not expected him to name her.

Philip gazed into the distance and wrung his hands together. "Are you disappointed?"

"Disappointed?" Michaela stood, shaking her head in disbelief. She turned to face him. "You're like a best friend to me—a brother."

He let out a short sigh and frowned. "I don't want to be a brother to you. I want much more than that. I want to ask you to marry me."

Philip wanted to marry her? Philip, who had been an anchor in her life since the fire, no longer looked at her as her husband's wife?

Ethen.

Michaela stopped suddenly as a wave of panic swept through her. How could she even think about loving someone else and betraying her husband's memory? "What about Ethen?"

Philip grasped the wooden post beside him and shook his head slowly. "Ethen's gone. He would want you to be happy again."

"I know, but. . ."

A slight grin played on Philip's lips. "At least you would know he approved of the man."

"You were his best friend." Her mind spun with the implications of what he was saying. Philip loved her and wanted a relationship with her. But was that something she could give him?

Philip held up his hand as if to stop her. "You don't have to say anything now; just think about it. You and me. We're so right for each other. It makes sense."

"Philip, if I ever fall in love again, I don't want to do it because it makes sense. I. . ." Michaela sat beside him and took his hands, squeezing them gently. "I'm sorry. You took me totally by surprise. You know I'm crazy about you, Philip, but I never thought about you—about us—being romantically involved."

"Never?" He frowned, and she could hear the disappointment in his voice.

"I'm sorry, but no. I don't know what to say. It's not you. I've just never thought about there being anyone else." Michaela struggled with her words. The last thing she wanted to do was to hurt him, but she also knew she had to be honest. "I think I want to get married again someday. I just don't know if I'm ready for that now. I'm not over Ethen yet. I still miss him so much."

"I know. Just promise me you'll think about the possibility of us together." He shrugged his shoulders and gave her a hopeful look. "Give me a chance. We could start over. I want to court you, Michaela. I want to take you out to dinner, buy you flowers, and escort you to church."

"Oh, Philip." Michaela stood and tilted her head. "You know, the funny thing is, you do all those things already. When did you realize you were in love with me?"

"The other day when you were upset about the board's

decision and we went out to dinner. You were smiling and laughing. You hadn't done that for so long, and I liked being the one to make you smile again. I want to be that person in your life."

Michaela walked over to one of the trees next to the swing and leaned against the rough bark. Philip meant so much to her. He had been there through the most difficult time of her life, and he continued to be there today. He was the one who'd told her Ethen and Leah were gone. He had stood by her at the funeral as the tiny casket was lowered into the ground beside her husband's. He had cried with her over the emptiness she felt. She knew he understood, because he had always been a part of her life and had felt his own loss of a brother and niece.

She also knew someday she wanted to find the right man, fall in love again, and get married, but she didn't know if that time had come yet.

They were both quiet for a few moments, until she finally broke the silence. "Philip, something happened while you were gone." She went back to the swing and sat beside him. "Maybe this isn't the best time to tell you, but you need to know, especially now. Emma is expecting another baby, and she's having a hard time. I decided to go help them out until the baby's born. I've already sent a telegram to my brother, and I'll be leaving next week."

"Don't go." He leaned closer, and she felt the desperation in his voice. "Don't you see? If we marry, we could adopt Anna. It would be perfect. Michaela, I know you care for me. You could come to love me."

He was right. If they married, they could adopt Anna and become a family. Wasn't that what she wanted? A family? Her breathing quickened at the torrent of emotions she faced. It seemed like such a logical solution. But what about love?

Finally, she shook her head, her eyes pleading with him to understand. "Philip, I can't marry you for those reasons. It just wouldn't be right. Please understand. I need some time to think."

"I'm sorry." He sat back again and raked his hand through his hair, undisguised pain evident in his eyes. "I don't want to pressure you. Things just seemed so clear to me all of a sudden."

"No, I'm glad you told me."

"Promise me one thing. When you come back, will you let me court you?"

Michaela thought for a moment, trying to interpret what her heart felt. "I can't make you any promises except that while I'm gone, I'll do a lot of praying. I realize I still need to let Ethen go so I can get on with my life. I don't know right now, but maybe it will be with you."

"Remember one thing, Michaela. I'll always be here for you. You know that, don't you? No matter what happens between us."

Michaela looked into his deep blue eyes and smiled. "That's one thing I will always know."

&

"I'm not surprised one bit," Aunt Clara said to Michaela as they washed the dinner dishes. "I've wondered for some time if Philip didn't care about you—in a way other than friendship, I mean."

"Why didn't you say something?" Michaela demanded as she set the last of the dishes in the cupboard.

Aunt Clara wrung the wet rag and washed the counter. "I wasn't sure he realized it himself, and besides, I may always play the part of the matchmaker, but something held me back when it came to the two of you."

Sitting at the small table, Michaela rested her chin in her hands. "How could you tell?"

"There was something in his eyes when he looked at you, the way he held your hand a little too long, and the way he smiled whenever you entered a room."

"You noticed all of that?" How could she have missed something that had been clear to Aunt Clara? "Why didn't I notice?"

"You're still in love with Ethen."

Michaela fell silent. Her aunt was right. How many other things had she failed to notice because she was still wrapped up in the past?

Aunt Clara shook out the dishrag and laid it across the sink before sitting beside Michaela at the table. "What you've been going through is normal, but at some point, you have to look forward instead of behind."

Michaela shook her head. The revelation of Philip's affections seemed more like a dream than reality. "I care about him, but I don't know if I could fall in love with him."

Aunt Clara reached over and put her arms around her niece. "When the time is right, and it's the right person, you'll know. Give it time."

≈

Philip wandered down the quiet street toward his home, wondering if he'd done the right thing in confessing his feelings toward Michaela. The pale moon shone above him, casting eerie shadows against the storefronts. He'd never felt uncertain about his future before. Spending the rest of his life with Michaela had seemed like the perfect solution.

But was that all it had been? Had he mistaken a possible marriage of convenience for love?

At his cabinetmaking shop, he took the steps two at a time and entered the empty room above the store. He'd lived here for seven years and never felt lonely—until now. He'd never met a woman he wanted to share his life with, raise a family with, and grow old with together. Now that he'd revealed his feelings to Michaela, she was leaving and would be gone for months. He felt at a loss—how was he to win her heart now?

He looked around the room. Discarded clothes lay across the back of a wooden chair. A pile of books had been scattered across the small table beside a mug of forgotten coffee. As a bachelor, he'd never needed much more than the basics. A few simple furnishings had been adequate, but an unfamiliar sense of longing overcame him.

He didn't know what reaction he'd expected from Michaela, though he would have welcomed a shared confession of love. Clearing the table, he laid the stack of books on the shelf and dumped the leftover coffee. Love from Michaela wasn't realistic at this point. His one fear was that his feelings for her, even if never returned, would affect the friendship that had developed between them. He loved her too much to let his feelings change what they had.

Marrying Michaela still seemed like the perfect solution— not just for the two of them, but for Anna as well. They could give her what she needed most—a family to call her own. And there could be more children as the years passed. His business did well enough for him to support a large family, if that was what Michaela wanted.

He sat on the edge of the bed and ran his fingers through his hair. What did Michaela want? That was the question that really mattered. He shouldn't have been surprised at the fact that she'd never thought of the two of them as something other than simply friends, but he'd dared to hope that once he declared his love, it would awaken unexplored feelings in Michaela's heart. The same thing he'd experienced when he looked at her that day in the wood shop with the sun streaming through her hair.

But there wasn't only their relationship he had to consider. In less than a week, Michaela was leaving. And where that left him, he had no idea.

≈

Michaela tossed and turned, trying to sleep after Philip's confession. She cared about him, but was it enough to build a marriage on? It had only been recently that she could admit to herself she might want to marry again—someday. Still, she didn't know how she could ever love someone as much as she loved Ethen.

Part of her wondered if God hadn't placed a second chance at love right before her eyes. Somewhere deep inside, she knew this wasn't the way. She could never marry Philip unless she knew she loved him with all her heart. If she married him now, she'd only be giving him second best.

five

A cool breeze blew outside, perfect for a summer day on the beach. Michaela studied her reflection in the bedroom mirror, wondering if the dress she chose was right for the outing. She had already tried on four others and still couldn't make up her mind. The yellow fabric hugged her waist and draped gracefully past her hips. Its fashionable leg-of-mutton sleeves and lacy collar made it a favorite of hers.

When Philip had asked her to spend the afternoon with him, she hadn't even hesitated in telling him she would love to. Their relationship had changed because of what he had told her, and it could never be the same again, but she still wanted to spend time with him before she left.

On Sunday at church, she had noticed some of the things her aunt had mentioned. The way he held her gaze longer than necessary and grasped her hand after helping her out of the carriage.

No, things could never be the way they had been before.

Michaela had expected to feel uncomfortable around him, but she didn't. It had been a long time since a man had looked at her and told her that he loved her. It felt good to be wanted again—to be cherished and desired.

"Michaela?" Aunt Clara knocked on the door and peeked in. "Philip's here."

"What about this dress?" Michaela smoothed her hands against the silky fabric, wondering again about the attire she had chosen.

"It's always been one of my favorites." Aunt Clara folded her arms across her chest and studied her.

"Mine, too, but—"

"Am I sensing a bit of nervousness on your part?" A grin broke out across Aunt Clara's face. "I hadn't expected this."

Michaela fell back against the bed and groaned. "I don't know how I feel. This whole thing with Philip took me by surprise. It's been a long time since I worried about how I looked, but for some crazy reason, I want to look just right today."

Aunt Clara sat beside her on the bed. "You look beautiful, and I know without a doubt Philip will agree with me."

"Do you remember when I first fell in love with Ethen?" Michaela sat up and straightened the collar of her dress.

"It seemed as if the two of you had been in love forever." A dreamy look crossed Aunt Clara's face, and Michaela wondered if her aunt was remembering when she first fell in love with Uncle Henry. "I remember when you realized how you felt."

"I was eighteen years old, and suddenly I took twice as long to get dressed whenever I knew I was going to see Ethen." Michaela faced the mirror and pulled her curls back into a large chignon, then ran her fingers through her short bangs. "He took me to a church picnic one Sunday afternoon. We had always been friends, good friends, but I hadn't really thought beyond that. I looked at him as we sat beside the lake and knew at that moment that I loved him and wanted to spend the rest of my life with him."

Aunt Clara shook her head slowly. "You seemed so young."

"But I'm not anymore. I'm thirty-two years old." Michaela stood and faced her aunt, her hands resting against her hips. "Oh, Aunt Clara, do you think someday I might be able to love Philip the way I loved Ethen?"

"I can't answer that, sweetheart." Aunt Clara wrapped her arms around Michaela and held her tight.

"I could have Anna." Michaela's heart churned inwardly. "If I marry Philip, we could be a family."

Aunt Clara cupped her hand on the side of Michaela's face. "I know how alone you've felt at times. Sometimes I wish I'd found someone else—someone to fill the lonely spot in my life. Someone to grow old with me and laugh at my jokes."

Michaela nodded, wishing it didn't have to seem so complicated—or was it? "Philip is comfortable and familiar. He knows me, and we'd be happy together."

"It's a choice you're going to have to make."

Michaela took a step backward and looked toward the door, needing a change in the direction of the conversation. "What about Ben White from church? I've seen the way he looks at you."

"Michaela!" Color rushed to Aunt Clara's cheeks, and she quickly changed the subject. "I think Philip's waited long enough."

Michaela tried not to laugh at her aunt's reaction and followed her down the narrow staircase and into the parlor where Philip waited for her. He stood when they entered the room.

"You look lovely." His gaze lingered on Michaela's face.

Aunt Clara cleared her throat. "I made a picnic lunch. Fried chicken, baked beans, cake, and lemonade."

"Sounds wonderful. Thank you." Philip picked up the food box Aunt Clara had prepared for them and turned to Michaela. "I have the buggy out front if you're ready."

Michaela kissed her aunt on the cheek. "We'll be back before dark."

"Enjoy yourselves," her aunt replied.

Michaela sat next to Philip in the buggy. Suddenly, she felt shy around him. His short, curly hair lay in dark waves across his head, and she couldn't help noticing how handsome he looked in his white shirt and dark blue pants. She let out a soft laugh, realizing how much time the two of them must have spent getting ready.

"All right." He turned and looked at her, his dark brows raised in uncertainty. "What is it? My hair, my clothes? You look as though you're about to burst."

"It's not you; it's us." She rested her fingers across her mouth, trying to stop the erupting giggles.

"What do you mean, it's us?"

"We've been friends for so many years, and we know just about everything there is to know about each other."

His brow creased. "And that's funny?"

"No. What's funny is I spent two hours getting ready this morning, and I know you did the same thing."

A ripple of laughter broke from his lips as he nodded in agreement. "Does that mean there's a chance for me?" A solemn grin quickly replaced his laughter. "For the two of us?"

"Let's give it some time." She felt a tug of emotion pull on her. "You've helped me find contentment and never let me forget that someone cares about me."

"I've always cared for you, Michaela."

"I know, but loving someone is different." She let her gaze wander down the street that bustled with the noise from other buggies and pedestrians. Love was a complicated issue. She turned her attention back to him, not wanting to hurt him but knowing she needed to be honest about how she felt. "I can't say that I'm in love with you, but I do know you've made me very, very happy."

"And I intend to keep on making you happy."

They were silent, and she knew they both realized the possibility of a relationship had come at a difficult time. Determined to put thoughts of leaving aside, Michaela smiled as Philip shyly reached for her hand and placed it safely in his own.

❧

"I love the sea." Michaela leaned back against a rock, pulling her knees against her chest. She took a deep breath and let the salty air fill her lungs. "It's so beautiful. Constant and yet ever changing at the same time."

Philip stood beside her, throwing pebbles into the tide as it rolled in a continuous motion. It was getting late. They would have to go back soon, but she didn't want the day to end. This would be the last day she'd spend with him for months.

"It's been a good day, hasn't it?" Philip took a seat beside her on the sand and stretched out his legs in front of him.

"It's been perfect. I can't remember the last time I spent a whole day doing nothing but relaxing."

"It's about time. Of course, it's been quite awhile since I took a day off as well. I guess we both need to learn to enjoy the beauty God's placed around us."

"What's your excuse?" Michaela dug the toes of her boots into the sand and watched the white spray of water as the incoming tide splashed against a small outcropping of rocks along the shoreline. "I'm running away from the past. What are you running from?"

Philip looked out across the ocean as if contemplating her question. "I don't know. My room's lonely at night, so I'd rather work than go home. It's something I've only been able to admit recently."

"Why haven't you ever married? I know I've tried more than once to set you up with someone."

Philip arched his arm backward, then threw another rock into the oncoming tide. "How could I forget? You and Ethen were always trying to get me hitched. Remember Sassy Winter?"

Michaela laughed at the forgotten memory. "I'll admit I was a bit out of line with her."

"A bit?" He nudged her gently with his shoulder. "She never quit talking during the entire dinner, and none of us could get a word in edgewise. Half of the time I didn't even know what she was talking about. What was it she was interested in?"

"Her father left her a rather large inheritance, and she spends it studying rare plants. From what I understand, she's really quite knowledgeable on the subject."

Philip shook his head. "Well, it was beyond me. In fact, it seems that most of the women I've met talk incessantly. Except for you, of course. You seem to understand that the amount of conversation is not equal to the level of intelligence."

She smiled at the compliment, and for a moment they both sat still, listening to the rhythmic sounds of the ocean and the occasional cry of a shorebird.

"Shall we walk for a bit?" He helped her up from her sitting position but didn't let go of her hand as they walked along the sand. "It isn't that I was in love with you when Ethen was alive. You were Michaela, the girl next door who married my brother. But now I realize what it really means to love someone. I never felt this way toward anyone before. I knew God's timing was always right and that one day I would meet someone, but little did I know that person had always been right here with me."

Michaela looked out across the gray-blue waters, not knowing what to say.

"I'm sorry. I promised I wouldn't pressure you, and the way I'm going on—"

She squeezed his hand. "You're not. I just have a lot to think about. You've always been there for me, and I don't want to lose you first of all as a friend. Part of me wishes I wasn't leaving for Cranton tomorrow."

"Don't." He stopped and rested his index finger against her lips to quiet her. "Don't talk about that now. Let's just enjoy the rest of today."

She closed her eyes and felt the gentle touch of his lips brush hers.

"Michaela. . ." He reached forward and kissed her again. This time his hands encircled her waist. As he drew her close, she felt herself melt into his embrace. This was what she wanted. She wanted him to hold her and tell her how much she meant to him. Part of her was certain this must be a dream, but as she looked into his eyes, feeling his warm touch and the smell of fresh cedar that lingered from his work at the shop, she knew it was real.

If only she could put the past behind her and let go of Ethen, she might be ready to love again.

☙

That night Michaela picked up the Bible she kept on the small table next to her bed and set it in her lap. In the morning she would board the train for the other side of Massachusetts. It might as well be the other side of the world.

The image of Philip seemed so real, his kiss so poignant,

that she felt torn between going to help her brother and sister-in-law and staying here with Anna and Philip. Emotions swirled within her, leaving her confused. Maybe it was best that she was going away for a while. It would give her time to sort out her feelings without any distractions. She couldn't say she loved Philip, at least not the way she had loved Ethen, but tonight when he kissed her, he'd stirred something within her that hadn't been awakened for a long time.

Sitting up in her bed with the thick, cream-colored quilt her mother had made over twenty years ago wrapped around her, she opened her Bible to the fourth chapter of Philippians. Pastor Simon, who had performed her wedding twelve years ago as well as the funeral for her husband and daughter, had shared with her this chapter. She'd almost worn out the page in the Bible, reading it whenever she needed encouragement. When she finished the first half of the chapter, she read the seventh verse again.

" 'And the peace of God, which passeth all understanding, shall keep your hearts and minds through Christ Jesus.' "

"God. . ." She struggled with the words to begin her prayer. "I hardly know what to say. I read of Your promises for peace and strength in Your Word, but sometimes You just seem so far away. How do I find this peace that passes understanding? The peace You promise?"

She closed her Bible and pulled the book tightly against her chest. "Sometimes I think I'm healing and getting my life back together; then I see the face of my little girl, and I don't understand why she had to die. I want to let go of the past, but I don't know how.

"And Ethen. . .I miss him so much, God. I feel lonely without him, so lost. We had plans for the future, and now they're all gone. Philip loves me, but I don't know if I can open up my heart to him. I don't know if I can let anyone inside. I know to love Philip isn't betraying Ethen, but I still find my heart holding back. And now losing Anna. . .O God, give me the strength and the courage to live again. Help me to remember You are near so I might once again find peace in my life. The peace that transcends all understanding."

Michaela lay her Bible down next to her on the bed and closed her eyes. Had she been letting God heal her, or had she instead been holding in her pain and refusing to let go of it? She knew she could never truly love Philip or anyone else until her heart healed.

❧

"Are you sure you'll be all right?" Michaela stood at the foot of her bed and voiced her fears to Aunt Clara, concerned she'd made the wrong decision in leaving. Her trunk was already packed and sitting beside the dresser, along with the two other small bags she planned to take.

"It's not like you'll be gone forever. Just until the baby is born and Emma gets back on her feet." Aunt Clara shook her head and smiled. "Besides, there are plenty of people at church who have promised to look in on me now and then."

"I know; it's just hard not to worry."

Her aunt cupped Michaela's face in her hands and looked deeply into her eyes. "You may not always feel this way, but the past few months have given you a strength that often comes through adversity. You're not going alone. God will go with you and sustain you. He has 'engraved each of us on the palms of His hands.'"

Michaela smiled and let her aunt's paraphrase of Isaiah 49:16 comfort her spirit. "You always know what to say."

"I know you're nervous, but I'll be fine and so will you. Is everything packed now?" Her aunt took a step back and glanced around the room. "Philip should be here shortly to take you to the station. I made him promise not to be a minute late."

"I just need to change my clothes and make sure I haven't forgotten anything."

Michaela studied her aunt, memorizing each feature. She loved her so much, from her wrinkled face that had always shown Michaela so much kindness to the white hair she wore in a neat bun at the base of her neck. She had been Michaela's mentor, her adviser, and most of all, her friend.

"I'm going to miss you so much, Aunt Clara." Michaela gave the older woman an affectionate hug as she tried unsuccessfully to stop the tears. "I wish you were coming with me."

"So do I. I'll miss you, but I'm too old and set in my ways, even for a trip across the state. You'll be back before you know it."

Michaela looked into Aunt Clara's eyes, praying that she would one day possess the same measure of godliness and wisdom.

"I believe this time away will be very important for you. Philip loves you very much, and nothing will change his feelings for you between now and when you come back. I'll go downstairs to watch for him while you finish getting ready."

Michaela sat on the bed and looked around the room that had been hers as a teenager and again when she moved back after the fire. It seemed silly to say good-bye to a room, but for some reason she needed to. It was a simple room filled only with a bed, armoire, dresser, and chair, along with a few things that helped give the room a homier look. If she decided to marry Philip when she came back, this room would once again be empty.

"Philip's here," her aunt called from downstairs.

Gently, Michaela closed the lid to the trunk. It was time to go.

☙

"You promised you'd write me," Philip reminded Michaela as he helped her out of the buggy once they reached the busy train station. The smell of burning coal hung in the air as passengers hurried across the platform or waited on long wooden benches for the next arrival.

"I haven't forgotten."

She was glad Philip had insisted on taking her to the station. She found herself holding on to the familiar, afraid it might change while she was away.

"I assured your aunt I would check in on her, so don't worry about a thing. She'll probably outlive us all." Philip smiled, causing her heart to skip a beat.

She laughed. "You're right."

"Six months is a long time." Philip set the trunk on the platform and handed her the tickets.

"The baby is due around Christmas, so if everything goes well, I'll be back the first of next year." She flinched at the words. It sounded like a lifetime away.

"That's forever." Philip reached out and brushed her cheek gently with his hand. "I love you with all my heart, but I'll wait for you as long as you need me to."

Michaela gazed into his eyes and knew that here was a man who loved her unconditionally—a man who wanted to spend the rest of his life with her. She prayed that someday she would be able to say the same of him.

The conductor called out, "All aboard!" and Philip reached down gently and cupped her face in his hands. As their lips met, Michaela found herself responding to his kiss. She lifted her arms around his neck and felt his hands tighten around her waist. She longed for him to hold her forever, never letting go. Finally, she backed slowly away from him, and without another word, she boarded the train.

six

Michaela woke to the sun peeking into Daniel and Emma's second-story guest room. Soft rays of light streaked across the pale green walls that matched to perfection the hand-made quilt on the bed. Crawling out from under the covers, she went and stood beside the window that overlooked the front yard. Several old trees stood tall, their twisted limbs swaying in the morning breeze. Beyond them lay pastures of grazing cattle, hillside orchards, and, eventually, the Connecticut River.

Her first week in Cranton had passed quickly. More than happy to jump in and take over the cooking and housework, she'd found little time to dwell on her loss of Anna or even the possibility of a future with Philip. Turning away from the window, she swept her hand across the smooth top of the pine dresser. Perhaps the truth was she simply hadn't allowed herself to imagine what her return to Boston might bring.

Her gaze moved across the room and rested on a rocking chair and empty bassinet. She wasn't the only one whose arms ached for the soft touch of a child. Daniel and Emma had never even been able to hold their babies. All they had left were two tiny grave markers. Someday, she prayed, this room would echo with the laughter of her brother's children.

Shaking off her melancholy mood, Michaela mentally went over her plans for the day. The church social was to take place today, and she was looking forward to meeting some of the people who lived in the area. She'd spent the previous day baking and planned to take two chocolate cakes and several loaves of fresh bread to the celebration.

After putting on a lavender dress with dark purple trim, Michaela hurried downstairs. The strong aroma of coffee filled the cozy room where Emma sat at the kitchen table reading her Bible. Her dark hair hung neatly in one long braid down her back with loose curls framing her face. Her dress, a deep chocolate brown, pulled tight across her stomach, showing the first signs of pregnancy.

"Good morning, Emma." Michaela smiled at her sister-in-law, glad to see that the color was back in her cheeks this morning. "You must be feeling better."

"I am." Emma glanced up from her Bible and returned the smile. "I thought the least I could do was get up early and make some coffee."

"It smells wonderful." Michaela poured herself a cup of the hot drink and took a long swallow. Despite the fact that Michaela had been unable to spend much time with Emma since she and Daniel had moved to Cranton, Michaela still considered Emma a close friend.

Emma shut the heavy book and walked toward the cupboard. "I know the doctor wants me to rest as much as I can, but I get so tired of staying in bed."

Michaela squeezed Emma's hand, knowing how much this child meant to her. "In a few months, when you're holding your baby in your arms, you'll forget all about the struggles you're going through right now."

"I know." Tears misted in Emma's eyes as she ran her hand across her abdomen in a slow, circular motion. "Sometimes I get so scared that I'll lose this one, too."

The ache in Michaela's heart intensified as she struggled with what to say. "I know how bad it hurts to have lost a child. Aunt Clara always reminds me how God has promised to go through the valleys with us and that He will carry us through times of trouble."

Emma wiped away a stray tear and let out a soft chuckle. "I don't know why I get so emotional. Daniel's always teasing me about how I'm laughing one minute, then crying the next."

"It's all right." Michaela handed her a clean rag from the counter.

Emma dabbed at her eyes with the cloth and let out a deep sigh. "I know you understand. That's one of the reasons I'm glad you're here." She waved her hands in front of her. "Enough of this. We have a celebration ahead of us."

"Do you feel well enough to come?" Michaela set a black iron skillet on top of the stove and pulled some potatoes from a wooden bin to start breakfast.

"I'm sure going to try. The Johnson farm isn't far away, so if I start to feel bad, Daniel can always bring me home."

Michaela set to work chopping enough potatoes to fry for the three of them. "I'm glad you're coming. It will do you good to get out of the house for a while."

"You're spoiling me, you know." Emma set three plates on the round table, then added the silverware.

"That's why I came."

"I didn't realize how much it would help me. Just knowing I don't have to worry about Daniel fending for himself is a great relief."

Michaela cracked an egg into a bowl, the corners of her mouth tilting into an affectionate smile. "It certainly doesn't look as if he's been starving."

"I heard that." The front door banged shut, and Daniel's deep laughter floated in from the front room. He stomped into the kitchen, leaving traces of mud across the recently mopped floor.

"How do you put up with this man?" Michaela set her hands on her hips as Daniel gave his wife a kiss on the cheek.

A rosy blush crept up Emma's face. "I thought somebody had to, so it might as well be me."

Michaela laughed. "You'd better go get washed up for breakfast."

Twenty minutes later, Daniel slid into his seat, and Michaela placed a steaming hot plate of eggs and potatoes in front of him. "You know, I've missed you, little sister."

"It has been way too long." She smiled at the familiar teasing that had always been a part of their relationship. "Emma, are you hungry?"

Emma waved her hand toward the stove and frowned. "I was going to try to eat, but I think I'll just have a dry piece of toast. That's about all I can handle this morning."

Daniel reached over and squeezed his wife's shoulder. "Ladies, we need to hurry if we're going to make it to the Johnson place before the celebration gets into full swing."

❧

"What a beautiful home." Michaela leaned forward in the wagon as Daniel pulled on the reins and stopped in front of the Johnsons' charming gray-shingled farmhouse, with its large porch and symmetrical front windows.

"The man in the black shirt is Eric Johnson," Daniel told Michaela as he helped her down from the wagon. "He and his wife had six children before she passed away a few years ago."

Eric Johnson leaned against the porch rail, his tall, lean

figure towering over most of the guests. Several children, whom she assumed to be his, played quietly nearby. Michaela wondered how a single man could raise such a large brood of kids, though each one of them looked properly cared for and well dressed.

She followed Emma to the house, then stopped for a moment, captivated by the man who stood before her. Taking a closer look at the farmer, she studied him. His broad shoulders were supported by his equally muscular frame, and he was tanned from hours of work in the sun. His hair, dark as coal, lay perfectly against his forehead.

"Michaela." His firm hand met hers as Daniel introduced them. "It's good to finally meet you. Emma and Daniel have told me so much about you."

"It's nice to meet you as well, Eric." Michaela noticed the dimple in his right cheek when he smiled. "Daniel's mentioned what a big help you've been to them."

"Just being neighborly." Eric rested his hand on the shoulder of the child closest to him. "Let me introduce you to my children, Mrs. Macintosh."

The smallest of the group ran up and grasped Michaela's hand. "My name's Ruby. I'm six, and I think your dress is beautiful."

Michaela bent down to give Ruby her full attention and was drawn to the little girl's dark brown eyes, long lashes, and radiant smile. "Thank you, Ruby. I'm very glad to meet you, too."

Eric let out a soft chuckle and proceeded to introduce the rest of the children. "This is Rebecca, my oldest."

Michaela stood to look at the rest of the children, still holding Ruby's hand. Rebecca wore her long hair in a simple twist, allowing two soft tendrils to escape, one on either side of her face.

"Hard to believe it," Eric continued, "but she just turned seventeen. She's a wonderful cook."

"It's good to meet you," Michaela said warmly to the young woman who had inherited her father's dark hair and striking good looks.

"I'm glad you could join us, Mrs. Macintosh."

"And this," Eric said, pointing to the next in line, "is Samuel. He's fourteen."

"Do you like frogs?" He pulled one out of his pocket and held it up to Michaela's face. She took a step back, then stifled a laugh at the slimy pet.

"Samuel!" Eric gave him a sharp look and pointed his son in the direction of the barnyard. "That belongs outside and not in your pocket. What do you say?"

The young boy hung his head and stared at the ground. "I'm sorry, ma'am. Sarah's a girl, and she likes frogs just like me. I thought you might like them, too."

Samuel marched off the porch to let his frog go, avoiding the stern look from his father. Despite the reprimand, Michaela was certain she saw a sparkle in Eric's eyes.

Eric cleared his throat and turned to the next child. "Matt, my youngest son, is twelve."

"Do you have something to show me as well?" Michaela asked, noticing his hands hidden behind his back.

"No, ma'am." Matt brought his hands out from behind his back and held them up.

Eric looked at his youngest boy and ruffled his hair. "Next," he continued, "is Adam. He's my right-hand man, I guess you could say. When I'm gone, he's in charge."

"How do you do, Adam?" It wouldn't be long until he was as tall as his father.

Adam pulled at the collar of his shirt. "Just fine, thank you, ma'am."

"Adam is sixteen, and last but not least is Sarah. She's my only blue-eyed beauty," finished Eric. "She takes after her mother's side of the family."

Sarah, with corn silk–colored hair to match her blue eyes and fair skin, looked as if she were about to burst.

"Isn't this the most exciting day?" Sarah took a step closer to Michaela and clasped her hands in front of her. "Except for Christmas when you get presents, of course. Personally, I think this is the best day of the year. There's so much good food and games and. . ."

Michaela was sure Sarah would have continued indefinitely if her father hadn't glanced in her direction. Sarah quickly closed her mouth.

"I'm looking forward to this day, too, Sarah." Michaela stifled a laugh. "How old are you?"

"Nine." Sarah gave her father a crooked grin, then looked away.

"Make yourself at home," Eric told Michaela. "I know there are quite a few people looking forward to meeting you."

Michaela followed Emma inside the house, her attention immediately drawn to the piano in the corner of the large room. The dark wood shone like it had just been polished, and Michaela longed for a chance to play, already missing the calming effect the music brought.

She crossed the hardwood floor past a grouping of chairs and colorful rugs. Two large windows with bright red gingham curtains gave the room a warm and welcoming atmosphere.

A stone fireplace took up most of the far wall and stood as the focal point of the room.

The women were finishing lunch preparations in the kitchen. Emma quickly made the introductions, and several commented on the cakes Michaela had baked for the festivities.

"I think I'll forget lunch and just have a thick slice of your cake, Michaela," said Mary, a young woman with a pleasant smile, as she shifted the infant on her hip.

"I think I'll join you," another woman who'd introduced herself as Mae chimed in.

"Tell us about Boston." Several of the women gathered around and listened for the response to Mary's request. "It's been forever since any of us have been to the city."

Michaela felt instantly welcome and at home with these women as she talked about her hometown and answered a variety of questions ranging from fashion to transportation to church. Before long, lunch was ready, and Michaela helped carry the dishes out to the backyard, where several tables had been set up.

Lunch was wonderful—chicken, beef, ham, and all of the trimmings. Michaela's cakes received rave reviews, and she promised to make another one for the next gathering. She ate until she could hardly hold another bite, and before she knew it, it was time to clean up again.

In the kitchen, Michaela was happy to be partnered with Rebecca, Eric's oldest daughter, in drying the dishes.

"Do you enjoy school?" Michaela asked.

"Very much." Rebecca's smile confirmed her answer as she handed a dry dish to Sarah. "My favorite subject is math. I'm thinking about becoming a teacher, though I also love to sew."

"My mother was a teacher."

"Where does she live?"

Michaela felt the slight aching of her heart as she fingered the towel between her fingers. "She died when I was fourteen."

"I'm sorry." Rebecca handed Michaela another dish to dry. "My mother died several years ago. I still miss her."

"I miss my mother, too."

They were both silent for a moment, until Michaela decided to ask another question. "How much more schooling do you have left?"

"This is my last year. Then I can work on my teacher's certificate." Rebecca reached for another dish from the soapstone sink and began to wash it. "Father's been very supportive. He even found someone to help out with the house so I could have time to go to school."

Michaela wondered about this man, Eric Johnson, who'd spent the last few years not only running a farm, but raising six children alone. She'd noted his relaxed manner during lunch as he mingled among his guests, making sure that everyone felt at home. Somehow, despite the tragedy of losing his wife and being forced to be sole provider and parent for his family, he seemed to have found a sense of peace.

Sarah nudged between Michaela and Rebecca and grinned like a conspirator. "Did Rebecca tell you she has a beau? His name's Jake, and he's here today."

"Sarah!" Rebecca gave her sister a firm look, and Sarah quickly closed her mouth. "Never mind about that. What do you do in Boston?"

"I teach piano lessons. I noticed you have a piano in the front room."

"Unfortunately, none of us knows how to play," Rebecca admitted.

Michaela laid down her towel and rested her hands against the counter, surprised at the revelation. "You can't be serious."

"My grandmother sent it out here on the railroad," Rebecca said with a laugh. "She thought it would help us become cultured. She thinks Pa should have moved us all to the city after Mama died. She's sure we're going to grow up unrefined and unsophisticated without the benefits of living in a large city like Boston."

"Rebecca." Michaela toyed with an idea that was forming in her mind. "I could teach you how to play the piano. I could teach all of you." Michaela handed the last dish to Sarah, whose eyes were almost as wide as the plate she now held.

"You'll teach us how to play the piano?" Sarah asked.

"I could come out every Saturday and teach you one at a time." The more she thought about it, the more she liked the idea.

Rebecca shook her head. "That seems like a whole lot of work, Mrs. Macintosh—"

"I love teaching, and what good is your piano sitting in there without someone to play it? Plus, I already miss my piano, and it would give me a place to practice."

"I'll have to ask Father, but it sounds wonderful." A wide grin covered Rebecca's face.

"I'm going to go ask him right now." Sarah's enthusiasm got the best of her, and she ran out of the kitchen in search of her father.

ও

"Come on, Mrs. Macintosh, it's baseball. You have to play," Sarah insisted a little while later.

Never being one to miss out on the fun, Michaela had followed Sarah and the others out into the open field behind the Johnsons' barn, despite the fact she had doubts about the whole thing—including how ladylike the game was.

"How can you live in the city and not know anything about baseball?" Eric leaned against the wooden bat and shot her a grin.

"Yes, come on, Mrs. Macintosh, it's fun." Sarah, who had followed Michaela around all afternoon, now pulled on her arm.

"I don't know anything about baseball," Michaela protested for the third time.

"It's easy!" Adam tossed the white ball into the air and caught it with one simple swipe of his hand.

"Daniel?" Michaela looked to her brother, hoping he would back her up.

"Come on. You can be on my team." He winked at her, obviously not planning to intervene.

Michaela groaned.

"It's simple." Adam stepped forward and attempted to give her a swift course on the game. "All you have to do is hit the ball and run around the bases, or if you're playing in the field, you try to catch the ball."

The first person up to bat was Eric. Michaela held her glove ready like Adam had shown her. He hit the ball and it bounced right toward her, rolling to a stop between her legs. She reached down to grab the ball, keeping Eric in her line of sight the entire time. He ran toward second base. She threw the ball as hard as she could. Adam ran for her off-centered throw, then tried to beat Eric to the base. She let out a soft groan. He was safe.

Ten minutes later, her team was called up to bat.

"You're up, Michaela," Daniel said when it was her turn.

They were winning, three to two, and Michaela had picked

up a few things about baseball along the way, but she still felt ridiculous standing at home plate with the bat grasped between her hands. She tried to remember everything she'd been told. *Bend legs, lean over slightly, watch the ball.* Eric, who was pitching for the opposing team, threw the ball at her and she swung.

"Strike."

She looked over at Daniel and the Johnson kids, who were cheering her on. Eric threw the ball again. This time Michaela thought she detected a slight smirk on his face.

"Strike."

Michaela took in a deep breath and stared straight at him. Inky black hair curled slightly over his ears, and dark stubble shadowed his square jaw. Their gazes met, and an odd sensation swept through her. Feeling off balance for a moment, she tried to shake the feeling. Determined to concentrate on the game, she sucked in her breath and raised the bat.

Eric threw the ball. She swung. A crack sounded from the bat, and a cheer went up from behind her as she stood there watching the ball fly toward second base.

"Run! Run!" someone screamed behind her.

Michaela threw down the bat, picked up the hem of her dress, and ran for her life.

꙳

An hour later, Michaela leaned against the rail of the Johnsons' front porch, enjoying the end of the sunset. The murmur of voices filtered into the night, joining the low croak of a lone frog. Fireflies danced in the distance, their soft glow shimmering in the murky twilight.

"It's a beautiful night, isn't it?"

Michaela jumped at the deep male voice and turned around. "Eric?"

He came and stood beside her, keeping an arm's length between them. "I'm sorry if I startled you."

"No, it's fine. I was just enjoying the sunset." She brushed a hair out of the corner of her mouth and looked up at him. Despite her height, he still towered over her.

Eric rested his palms against the rail and leaned forward. "My mother always said that sunsets were gifts from God that should be shared."

She smiled at the expression. "I like that."

"Then you don't mind if I join you for a few minutes?"

"Of course not." Michaela watched the breeze tug at his hair and brush the top of his collar, then shifted her gaze to the orange and yellow of the sunset. "This has always been my favorite time of the day. Just before evening fades into night, and there's still a splash of color across the sky."

"I have to agree. It's beautiful." He cleared his throat and glanced at her. "Sarah tells me you offered to give the children piano lessons."

Shadows masked his expression, and she suddenly wondered if she'd made a mistake in agreeing to teach the children without talking to him first. "I hope I wasn't out of line."

"No, I didn't mean that." He angled his body toward her, one elbow still resting against the wooden rail. "What I meant was that six kids is a lot of lessons."

"It's something I really enjoy. Plus, it's a pity to have such a beautiful instrument that no one plays."

He let out a soft chuckle. "I have to agree with you on that one. If you're sure you wouldn't mind, I would be happy to pay you—"

"I'm not looking for a source of income." Michaela wondered if she'd left the wrong impression. "It really is something I enjoy. Just let me play it every once in a while and I will be more than happy. Are Saturdays all right with you?"

"Saturdays would be perfect."

Eric watched as Michaela pulled her embroidered shawl around her shoulders and tried to interpret the torrent of unfamiliar feelings that rushed through him. All afternoon, he'd been aware of her. Then when she'd caught his gaze on the baseball field, something had awakened within him.

Six years ago, he'd lost Susanna. She'd been the love of his life, and there hadn't been a woman since who'd captured him the way she did.

Then today, Michaela Macintosh had stepped out of the wagon, and, somehow, her laughter and bright smile had found a way into the recesses of his heart. He'd watched her interact with his children and the other guests—like this was the place she belonged. He shook his head at the image. For six years he and his children had worked the land, harvested the crops, and built up a farm to be proud of. Nothing needed to change.

Or did it?

"When we first moved out here, the town was no bigger than a whistle stop on the railroad line." Eric spoke and tried to get his mind off her silky red hair and soft, fair skin. "Since then, it's grown to become a viable place of trading and business."

The sun had sunk into the horizon, and the light of the moon captured her face. He caught her grin, and she laughed. "You forget I'm from Boston."

He shook his head and smiled. "In my mind, Boston can't compare to quiet nights like this. Here we have the best of both worlds."

"You do have a point. I have to admit I do find this part of the country very beautiful."

Daniel stepped out onto the porch behind them. "Michaela? I'm sorry to interrupt you. Emma needs to go home. She's exhausted."

"Of course. I just need to gather my things." Michaela pulled her embroidered shawl tighter around her shoulders and turned to Eric. "It's been a wonderful day. Thank you."

"I'm glad you could come." Eric followed them into the front room, disappointed she had to leave so soon. "The next time there's a baseball game, I'm going to insist on being on your team."

"My double play was simply beginner's luck." She laughed, then caught his gaze. For the second time that day, something passed between them. The color of her eyes had darkened from a pale icy blue to a deep indigo. For a brief moment, he found himself lost in them—but this was a place he wasn't sure he could afford to stay.

He tried to push away the emotion. He didn't have time for someone like Michaela in his life. In fact, he didn't need someone else. While certainly not perfect, his children were well adjusted, and his life was complete. He blew out a long sigh and watched as she drove away in Daniel's buggy. If that were true, then why did his heart suddenly feel a deep twinge of emptiness?

ஐ

At the farmhouse, Michaela got ready for bed, attempting to shove aside Eric's lingering image. When he'd looked at her, his dark brown eyes had seemed to pierce through to the deep alcoves of her heart—to a place she wasn't ready to let anyone enter.

Heaving a sigh, Michaela yanked a sheet of paper out of the desk drawer, then slammed it shut. She'd write Philip a long letter. Maybe there she could lose herself in what was comfortable and familiar. Quickly filling the page, she told him about her first week in Cranton and asked if he'd delivered Aunt Clara's dresser or had a chance to check on Anna.

Writing had the calming effect she desired. Just like Philip's presence always had. She had no doubt if she decided to marry him she would be happy. But what about love? That was the question she had to answer.

seven

Leaving the small church building where she and Daniel had attended the Sunday morning service, Michaela settled back in the buggy for the ride home. Fall had arrived, and with it a spectacular visage of color as the trees exploded into vivid shades of autumn. A measure of peace enveloped her as she enjoyed the beauty of the endless acres of farmland, towering green pines, apple orchards, and maple sugar houses scattered across the valley.

She'd enjoyed seeing the Johnson children again and, as at previous times, was amazed at their well-mannered behavior. There had been a few whispers between the siblings during the service, but a sharp glance from their father had stopped the misbehavior before it got out of hand. Even little Ruby, who was dressed in a darling lavender pinafore, had managed to sit through the minister's long lesson without much difficulty.

Two weeks ago, Michaela had begun teaching piano lessons at the Johnson home, and she was pleased with the children's interest. Adam and Sarah, in particular, possessed some musical talent, though her biggest challenge was to get Sarah to sit still long enough to take her lesson.

Daniel cleared his throat and guided the one-horse buggy onto the road that led to his farm. "I couldn't help noticing that a few of the single men were being extra friendly toward the new girl in town."

"Daniel!" Michaela's eyes widened in disbelief at her brother's comment.

"You have to admit, it was kind of obvious." Daniel let out a deep chuckle and shook his head. "I thought Joel Lambert was going to get a crick in his neck from turning around so many times. And Hiram Williams; that man had stars in his eyes when he looked at you."

Michaela folded her arms across her chest, unwilling to accept his assessment of the morning worship service. "I don't believe a word of what you're saying, but if anyone does ask, you'll have to spread the news that I didn't come here to find a husband."

"Then they're going to be some unhappy fellows."

Michaela ignored her brother's last comment, half wishing Emma had felt up to coming to church so she could help set Daniel straight. Michaela's brother had always been a tease, but this was a subject she'd rather not discuss.

She should have mentioned what had happened between her and Philip before she left Boston, but each time she thought about telling them, something held her back. If she didn't understand her own feelings toward him, how could she begin to explain their relationship to someone else?

"What about Eric Johnson?" Daniel raised his brows. "Not only is he a successful businessman, but he's a strong Christian as well."

Michaela heard the blatant implications of his question as Daniel tried to take on the role of matchmaker. It wasn't the first time Daniel had presented Eric in a good light.

Despite the fact she'd determined to forget the perceived attraction she'd felt the first day they'd met, Daniel's comments did ring true. Eric appeared to be an outstanding member of the community. She also hadn't missed the interested looks given by several of the single women after services as he strode by their circle.

A tiny black bug landed on her forearm, and she flicked it away. "I've enjoyed spending time with his children. While I'm sure they all have difficulties at times, they really are quite well behaved. Rebecca, for example—"

"I wasn't asking about his children." Daniel turned his head toward her and sent her a knowing glance before he turned his attention back to the road in front of them. "I wanted to know what you thought about their father. He's rather good looking, don't you think?"

Michaela felt the heat rise in her cheeks, and she turned her head away from Daniel. They passed a large house that was set back from the road and surrounded by towering pines and the huge white blossoms of hydrangea bushes. She studied the rough stone columns of the house and the long porch that would be a welcome shelter in the summer months, then considered his question.

Yes, she'd noted Eric's striking dark features. His eyes were the color of coffee, and when he smiled, his entire face lit up. Each step he took was marked with the confidence of a man who knew who he was and where he was going. She also wondered about his past sorrows. He'd lost his wife at a young age and had been left to raise their children alone. A situation like that could destroy a family, yet on the outside he appeared stronger because of it.

"I suppose one could say he's handsome, now that you mention it." She kept her voice even-toned. "But I'm not interested."

Daniel turned and looked at her. "If you're not interested

in getting to know anyone here, what about back home? Any suitors lurking in the wings?"

Michaela hesitated. "Maybe."

"I'm sorry." Daniel reached over and squeezed her hand. "I promised Emma I'd stay out of any form of matchmaking. It's just that I hate to think you might be lonely."

"I stay too busy to be lonely."

The shrill cry of a bird called out above them, breaking through the relative quiet of the afternoon. Why hadn't she mentioned Philip to her brother? He was a wonderful man who would make a fine husband for someone—for her—if she chose to say yes to his marriage proposal. Maybe it was time to tell Daniel the truth.

"There is someone. . . ."

He shot her a surprised glance. "You don't sound very sure."

"You remember Philip, Ethen's brother?"

"Of course."

Michaela brushed a piece of lint off her skirt, wondering why Philip's proposal still seemed surreal to her. "He asked me to marry him before I left to come here."

"Did you give him an answer?" Daniel's brows rose in question.

"I haven't yet. It all came about rather suddenly. I've always felt close to Philip, but I've seen him more as a brother. And since Ethen died. . .I've just never thought about anyone else."

"And now?" Daniel asked.

"Before I left, I began to seriously consider his proposal."

Daniel shrugged, shaking his head. "Then why did you come out here?"

Why did the situation seem so complex? "I needed to

come. He's sure of his feelings toward me, but I needed some time to think about things. Some time to get away and put the past behind me."

Daniel's warm hand embraced hers. "Then I hope you find what you're looking for while you're here."

&

"Mail call!"

Three days later, Daniel arrived from town with not only the sugar and other items Michaela had requested, but a letter from Philip as well. She took the bacon she was frying off the stove and sat down at the table before tearing open the envelope.

"I'll leave you alone." Daniel sampled a piece of the meat, then left to check on Emma.

My dearest Michaela,

It's only been a short time since you left Boston, but it feels like it's been much longer. I pray that you are adjusting well to life in Cranton and are enjoying the time you have with Daniel and Emma.

I also pray that I wasn't too forward in telling you the truth about my feelings. I never imagined that our relationship could ever be anything more than that of a close friendship. But I will also never regret the change that has taken place in my heart. Please know that I only want what's best for you, and whatever your decision concerning our relationship, I will accept it without question.

I spoke briefly with Aunt Clara after church last Sunday. . . .

Michaela could hear Philip's voice as he continued to describe how Ben White had finally found the courage to ask her aunt out to dinner, and how Vivian had announced her engagement to Charles Randolph, a fact that didn't surprise Michaela at all. Charles Randolph was the son of one of the city's bankers and very well-to-do. Many people from church sent their regards, especially Caroline, who never failed to ask about her.

> *I visited Anna yesterday and she's doing well. She asked about you and wanted me to tell you she misses you. I wish I didn't have to tell you this, but I spoke to Agnes as well. There's a family who's decided they want to adopt Anna. . . .*

Michaela reached the last paragraph and drew in a sharp breath, her heart breaking at the news.

"What is it, Michaela?"

She glanced up from the letter. Emma stood in the doorway of the kitchen.

"It's Anna." Michaela pinched the bridge of her nose with the tips of her fingers, trying to hold back the tears. "I knew this was coming, but I didn't realize it would happen so soon."

She stood and walked over to the large window that framed a view of the cornfields. "Philip spoke to Agnes. A family has decided to adopt Anna."

Emma came and rested her arm across Michaela's shoulders. "I'm so sorry. I know how much she means to you."

The well of sadness seemed to deepen with each second that passed. Anna had found a home, and it wasn't with her.

❧

An hour later, Michaela picked up two half-full buckets of milk and carried them out of the stall. She'd wanted to be alone with her thoughts, and the best place she could think of was the barn. Besides, Betsy and Maude needed milking.

She'd spent the past hour in prayer, and still the pain rippled through her, as fresh as when she first read the news about Anna.

I should be happy for her, Lord. Happy Anna will have a mother and a father. . . Happy because once again she'll have a place she can call home.

But she wasn't. How could she be happy when she knew she'd just lost Anna forever? Michaela shut the gate behind her and walked toward the house.

In a split second, Michaela found herself facedown in a mixture of mud and warm milk. She sat up and glanced around, thankful no one had seen her fall. Standing up, she stepped gently on the wet ground to make certain she hadn't sprained anything.

All right, Lord. Are You trying to test my sense of humor? If You are, it's not likely to please You today!

Michaela picked up the two empty buckets and carried them toward the house, setting them on the porch. Not wanting to track mud into the house, she quickly decided she'd need to take off her boots and dress.

Emma was asleep, and Daniel had left to work in one of the fields and wouldn't be back for several hours, so no one would see her. She sat on the steps and began to remove her boots, then heard someone call her name.

Michaela jerked her head up, dismayed to see Eric Johnson pulling up in the wagon.

"Of all days," she mumbled, knowing she must be a sight in her mud-streaked outfit. There was no escaping an encounter with their neighbor.

"Eric." Michaela forced a smile to cover her growing sense of frustration.

What else do You have in store for me today, Lord?

Eric stifled a laugh, which only fueled Michaela's anger. She shoved a stray wisp of muddy hair out of her eye.

"I guess there's no need to ask what happened," he said finally, "though I'm not sure if it was the pigs or—"

"It was not the pigs." She gritted her teeth and prayed he wouldn't make a joke out of it.

"I'm sorry."

Michaela took a deep breath to calm her nerves. She was not only mad about making such a fool out of herself but upset with Eric for showing up at the worst moment possible. She clenched her jaw, determined not to say what was on her mind.

"I shouldn't have laughed—"

"I really don't see the humor in all of this," she spouted, wanting to run inside the house. Her temper thundered within her, in sharp contrast to the tranquil, cloudless sky above her.

Michaela glared at him, then looked down at her mud-streaked form. Wiping her hands across the bodice of her dress, she let out an unladylike chortle. "I guess I do look a bit ridiculous, don't I?"

"I really am sorry," Eric said, still unable to hide his grin.

Michaela took another look at her grimy dress. Uncontrolled laughter bubbled out of her mouth. The tension broken, Eric looked at her wide-eyed for a moment. Soon they both were laughing until tears streamed down their faces.

Drawing the back of her hand across her cheek, she cleared her throat and attempted to compose herself. "You never said why you stopped by."

Still smiling, Eric shifted in the wagon seat. "I'm on my way into town to pick up some supplies, and I wondered if you needed anything. Besides soap."

Michaela snickered and shook her head. "Daniel went early this morning, so I can't think of anything."

He took off his hat and nodded his head. "You'll be all right then?"

She laughed again and nodded. "I'm fine."

"Then I'd better get going."

"Michaela?" Emma's voice sounded from inside.

"I'll be right in, Emma." Michaela wiped at a muddy spot on the sleeve of her dress, then turned back to Eric. "I need to go get cleaned up."

"Of course. I'll see you later."

Moments later, Michaela climbed up the stairs, abandoning her boots and ignoring the empty buckets on the porch.

"What happened?" Emma asked as she stepped out onto the porch.

"I slipped in the mud right before Eric showed up." Michaela ignored her sister-in-law's knowing glance. "He was simply on his way to town and stopped by to see if we needed anything."

Michaela followed Emma into the house, forgetting the mud dripping on the freshly cleaned floors and remembering only Eric Johnson's penetrating gaze.

❧

Eric left Daniel's farm with a smile on his face. It had been a long time since he'd met a woman like Michaela Macintosh. She was beautiful, funny, and intelligent. He'd seen the interested looks of several of the women at church directed at him, but not one of them had captured his attention like Michaela. And the fact that she had caught his attention surprised him.

He'd been lonely since Susanna's death, but the children and the farm kept him busy. There simply hadn't been a lot of time to grieve and long for what could have been. Slowly, the heartache had lessened as the pain from her passing began to ease.

A flock of nighthawks flew above him, their wings beating through the sky with apparent ease. As they passed overhead, he thought about the journey before them as they headed toward the coast, then on to an endless summer farther south. Life was about change. Nothing stayed the same. The Bible talked about change and a time for everything. A time to be born and a time to die. . .a time to weep and a time to laugh. . .a time for love. . .

Eric flicked the reins, urging his horses to pick up their pace. He'd never seriously considered courting again, but he'd also never met a woman he thought he might enjoy getting to know. There was something about Michaela that made him curious to find out what she thought about life. She was obviously generous and kindhearted. She'd shown that by her generosity in teaching his children. Life hadn't been easy for her, and yet from all outward appearances, she'd not let it turn her bitter.

Maybe he didn't need a woman in his life to ensure his family survived, but didn't he long for the companionship of a partner and spouse? The image of Michaela's slender form streaked with mud brought a smile to his face. He'd seen the red hue that brushed across her cheeks at his presence. Even caught in an embarrassing situation, she'd managed to appear poised. For the first time in years, Eric wondered if he should let his heart take a risk—and maybe Michaela was the woman he'd take that risk with.

eight

The following Saturday, after the breakfast dishes were washed and put away, Michaela saddled up Honey and headed over to the Johnson farm. The wind blew through the trees, lending a pleasant coolness to the early fall morning. Emma had been feeling particularly well these past few days and had shooed Michaela out the door, promising her that Daniel would be close by all day and able to help her if she needed anything.

During the past few days, Michaela had spent every waking moment cleaning and cooking—anything to keep her mind off Anna's adoption. Times of prayer had come interspersed with tears of frustration. She knew God had a plan for her life, but she longed for His confirmation of what that was.

"Mrs. Macintosh!" Sarah jumped off the porch steps and ran toward Michaela with Ruby in tow. "Rebecca said if it was all right with you, we could give you a tour of our house today before lessons."

As soon as Michaela had secured her horse, Sarah grabbed her hand and hurried toward the front porch. "You've never seen our room."

Michaela laughed quietly, certain Sarah's suggestion was simply a way to delay her lesson. The previous week, it had been obvious that Sarah had not practiced her scales during the week, and more than likely the same would hold true for this week.

"Make it quick," Rebecca said to the girls after greeting Michaela with a broad smile. "We can't keep Mrs. Macintosh here all day."

Sarah and Ruby each took one of Michaela's hands and led her into the house.

"Did we ever tell you that Father built the house?" Sarah's voice bubbled with her usual excitement. "Each year he added on until it was big enough for all of us."

Michaela followed the girls up the narrow staircase to the second floor, the one section of the house she'd never seen.

"There are four bedrooms upstairs," Sarah informed Michaela. "Ruby and I share a room." Sarah wrinkled her nose and stuck out her bottom lip, apparently not thrilled that she had to share a room with her little sister.

The girls led her to a room where there were two small beds with pink and white matching quilts and a simple pine dresser. White lace curtains hung gracefully on the window that overlooked the front yard, and several hooked rugs lay scattered about the floor.

"This is our room." Ruby threw herself atop her bed and grinned.

"It's beautiful." For a moment, all Michaela could see was Leah's room. Ethen had painted the walls pink, and she'd hand-stitched the quilt from scraps Aunt Clara had given her. She'd planned to make a quilt for Anna's room, but now someone else would fill that place in Anna's life.

Rebecca called up the stairs, drawing Michaela out of the past as she followed the two sisters back downstairs. Rebecca stood in the kitchen drying dishes. Determined to shove aside the ache in her heart, Michaela complimented her on the house.

"Rebecca did most of the decorating," Sarah said. "Father says she has a knack for it."

Rebecca tousled her younger sister's hair, then wiped her hands on a white apron embroidered with tiny yellow flowers along the bottom. "Our mother did most of it. I've just added a few things." Rebecca pointed to a fresh loaf lying on the counter. "She's the one who taught me how to cook. I thought you might like a piece later."

"I'd love one." Michaela smiled, savoring the pleasant aroma of ginger that filled the air.

She studied Rebecca for a moment, impressed at how she was able to help manage the household at such a young age. She had her father's brows and the same expressive eyes that seemed to smile when she was happy. Her long black hair had been parted in the center, then pulled back smoothly and arranged into a simple chignon, leaving a frame of bangs to soften the look.

At first Michaela had been afraid that in offering to give them piano lessons, Rebecca might feel defensive, but instead Rebecca seemed to yearn for the chance to develop a friendship with her.

Rebecca drew her arms around Sarah and held her tight. "You're first this morning." Rebecca glanced up at Michaela to explain. "We drew numbers last night to decide the order."

By the end of the morning, Michaela had given each of the children thirty minutes of lessons and had eaten several pieces of homemade bread with ice-cold lemonade. Ruby, her last student for the day, slipped outside as soon as her lesson was over, leaving Michaela to gather up her music.

"How are they doing?"

Michaela glanced up from the piano bench. Eric stood

casually in the doorway, causing her to wonder how long he'd been standing there. The heat in her cheeks rose as she remembered the last time he'd seen her, covered in mud.

"Your children show talent." She stood slowly, stretching the muscles in her back that had tightened after sitting for so long. "And if not talented, they certainly have energy and enthusiasm."

"My children will never be accused of being dull or boring." Eric stepped into the room and leaned against the back of a cushioned chair, folding his arms across his chest. "I wanted to thank you for what you're doing. It's always seemed like such a waste to have a piano no one could play."

"Hopefully that will change, but I have to warn you. They have to practice, which means months of scales and mistakes."

"I think we can deal with that."

The intensity of his expression made her heart race unexpectedly. Michaela turned back toward the piano, inwardly fighting her reaction to his presence. Letting out a deep sigh, she quickly gathered the music into her arms. What was it about him? Had it simply been too long since she'd spent time in the company of a man other than Philip or Daniel? Still, the effect he had on her was disturbing.

"Mrs. Macintosh, would you like to stay for lunch?" Rebecca asked as she stepped into the front room, her hands clasped behind her back.

Michaela gave her a smile of regret. "I appreciate the offer, but I really do need to head home." She pulled the music against her chest and took a step toward the door. "Maybe another time."

Rebecca thanked her again for the lesson, then went back into the kitchen, leaving her and Eric alone again for the moment. He followed her outside, his towering profile a strong presence.

"How's Emma doing?" Eric's long stride took the porch steps two at a time. "How's she feeling?"

Michaela slowed her pace. "The doctor says she's doing well, but I know they both would appreciate your continued prayers."

"I certainly will." Eric untied the lead rope on her horse and brought the animal to her. "I know they're both grateful you're here right now. Daniel wanted to plant some extra crops this fall, and it will be easier with you helping to care for Emma."

She shoved her music into her leather bag. "I'm actually a city girl, but I have to admit, this valley is growing on me."

"City life never was for me." Eric scuffed the toe of his boot in the dirt and smiled. "I spent one summer in Boston, and that was enough to convince me to never return. I wouldn't be surprised if after Emma's baby comes you decide to stay."

She shook her head and ran her fingers down the horse's mane. "I have a life waiting for me back in Boston."

Eric held out his hands, and after hesitating briefly, Michaela allowed him to help her into the saddle. A tingle of anticipation raced through her. For the first time since she'd arrived, Boston and Philip seemed a world away.

❧

A knock on the kitchen door drew Michaela away from the bread she was kneading. Rebecca stood on the back porch, shivering in her long-sleeved dress.

"Rebecca, come in." Michaela ushered the young woman to a chair beside the warm stove. "Where's your coat?"

Even in early October, the temperature had begun to drop

in the late afternoon, and though the sun had yet to set, the wind brought a brisk coolness with it.

"I wasn't thinking." Rebecca leaned closer toward the stove, warming her hands for a moment.

"Is something wrong?" Michaela left the bread and sat down beside her, trying to read her troubled expression.

"It's Father." Rebecca met Michaela's puzzled gaze. "He's furious with me."

Michaela wondered how Eric would feel if she got involved in something between the two of them. It certainly wasn't her place, yet if Rebecca trusted her enough to come to her, she couldn't send the young woman away. "Do you want to tell me what happened?"

"It's Jake Markham." Rebecca chewed on her thumbnail. "He's sweet on me, and, well, I guess you could say I feel the same about him."

Michaela smiled at the picture of young love, remembering the time when she first fell for Ethen. Her aunt and uncle had been extremely cautious at first, and Rebecca was even younger than she had been.

"He thinks you're too young?"

Rebecca nodded. "The problem is, if I were thirty, I'd still be too young."

Michaela chuckled at the unrealistic image of Eric locking his daughters away for the rest of their lives. "I suspect that if you give him some time to get used to the idea, he'll be extremely supportive."

Rebecca leaned her elbows against the table and rested her chin in the palms of her hands. "Maybe, but it's just so hard to talk to him about boys and womanly matters. He doesn't understand."

"It's hard for fathers to let their little girls grow up." Michaela's heart ached for the young woman, knowing full well how difficult it was to grow up without the love and comfort of a mother.

Rebecca blew out a sharp breath. "Jake came by this morning to ask Father if he could court me."

"What did your father say?"

"He said absolutely not." Rebecca slapped the palms of her hands against the table and leaned forward. "He said we can discuss the subject after I finish school. You have no idea how humiliating it was."

Michaela stood and went back to kneading the bread, giving herself time to think. She remembered the intense feelings she felt toward Ethen as well as Aunt Clara's questioning her readiness to marry. "You've made bread before."

"Of course." Rebecca's brow rose in question.

Michaela continued to knead, pushing down the dough with the palm of her hand against the wooden board. The pungent smell of yeast permeated the room. "When you first mix the ingredients together, it takes a bit of time for the flour, milk, and sugar to mix together and become soft and pliable."

"I suppose."

Michaela formed the dough into a ball, then set it into a bowl. "Give your father some time to get used to the idea that you're growing up. He'll let you, but he loves you very much and simply wants what is best for you."

"What if I don't agree with what's best for me?" Rebecca let out a soft chuckle. "What if he wants to make me into a loaf of white bread and I'd rather be a pan of sweet cinnamon rolls?"

Michaela brushed the loose flour off her hands, smiling at the image. "Raising children is not easy, but you're blessed to have a father who loves and cares for you."

"I know." Rebecca fiddled with a loose thread on her sleeve and frowned. "It's just that sometimes I think if I had a mother, it would be much easier to talk to her about. . .certain things."

Michaela sat beside Rebecca and squeezed her hand. It seemed natural to talk to her like a daughter—except she must never forget that role was not hers. "I'm always here whenever you want to talk, but give your father a chance to be there for you. He loves you."

ða.

Michaela stepped out of Daniel and Emma's warm farmhouse and into the brisk November weather. Shivering, she quickly saddled Honey and headed into town. With Christmas only a few weeks away, she needed to shop for gifts.

Despite the chilling wind that blew across the valley, she enjoyed the short trip into Cranton. Lazy brooks weaved between a patchwork of farms and the jagged confines of stone fences, reminding her she was miles away from the bustling sounds and smells of Boston.

Soon the clattering of hooves and voices drifted toward her as the town came into view. After securing Honey's lead rope to a post outside the general store, Michaela hurried inside, thankful for the warmth from the woodstove in the corner. She wouldn't find the selection she was accustomed to in Boston, but Mr. Cooper made sure the shelves were stocked for the Christmas holiday.

After greeting Mr. Cooper's daughter-in-law, Meredith, who stood idly behind the counter engrossed in a dime novel, Michaela began her search for appropriate gifts. Changing her mind several times, she finally made her selection—a lovely brooch for her aunt, two pairs of gloves for Daniel and Philip, and a hand-embroidered shawl for Emma.

Michaela couldn't resist buying a small coat and hat for Emma's baby. She wished she were a better seamstress and could have made things for everyone, but this would have to do.

Next she picked out a small doll for Anna and some candy wrapped in bright paper and ribbons for each of the Johnson children. She made her way toward the front of the store and laid her gifts on the counter.

"How's Emma?" Meredith pulled a pencil from the dark bun on the top of her head and tallied the purchases.

"She's doing well. The baby's very active, which the doctor says is a good sign."

The two women chatted for another minute until Michaela paid her bill and placed her purchases in the leather pouch she'd brought with her. Putting her gloves on, she hurried out to Honey.

At the sound of footsteps behind her, Michaela looked up to see Eric. He took off his Stetson, revealing his dark, tousled hair. She studied his black shirt and well-fitting trousers, trying to ignore the unwelcome stirring of her heart at his nearness.

"Michaela, how are you?"

He smiled, and she refocused her gaze to his face, but even there, the dark brown recesses of his eyes seemed to reach into places in her soul she didn't want him to find. "Fine, thank you. Just finished my Christmas shopping."

"Isn't it a bit early for that?"

She shivered as a cold gust of wind blew across her face. "I need to send some gifts to Boston, and I want to make sure they get there in time."

"Then I guess it's not too early." He rotated the brim of his hat between his hands. "I was just about to get a hot cup of coffee at the hotel. Would you care to join me?"

Michaela hesitated, then nodded. It would be nice to warm up before heading home.

The waitress seated them at a small table in the corner of the restaurant and told them she would bring their coffee right away. A dozen tables with blue-checkered tablecloths surrounded a large stone fireplace that kept the room comfortable in spite of the cold outside.

"I have to tell you how much I've been enjoying teaching your children," Michaela said when the waitress left.

Eric rubbed his hands together and blew on them. "We have our share of conflicts, but they're wonderful children."

Michaela took off her gloves and laid them on the table. "Do I detect a bit of pride in your voice?"

"A whole lot, actually." Eric smiled, and the dimple she'd noticed the day they met reappeared.

The waitress set two steamy cups of coffee in front of them. Michaela warmed her hands on the hot mug, surprised at how her feelings of nervousness had dissolved. "Daniel has told me how much things have changed in Cranton since you arrived."

"We certainly didn't have anything as nice as this." He shook his head slowly. "Hard to believe it's been almost eighteen years. When Susanna and I came out here, we had little more than the clothes on our backs and a dream of a better life to keep us going."

"She must have been beautiful. Your children certainly are." Michaela took a sip of the coffee, enjoying the warmth that flowed through her body.

"Susanna Elizabeth Stevens. That was her maiden name.

She told me it wasn't until she was five that she could pronounce her whole name." He chuckled at the memory. "And you're right, she was beautiful."

For a moment, his gaze drifted toward the fireplace, seemingly lost within the crackling flames. "Sometimes, for just a moment, I forget she's gone; then it all comes back to me."

"I'm sorry. You don't have to talk about it if you don't want to—"

"That's all right." His smile returned, replacing the momentary look of sadness. "We had a good life, full of happy memories. I like talking about her."

Sensing his desire to share, she encouraged him. "Please go on."

He leaned back in his chair and folded his arms across his chest. "Our parents knew each other before we were born, so we grew up together on Nantucket Island. Her father was a retired captain of a whaling vessel. Mine was a minister. We married at eighteen. Too young in many ways, but we were committed until death do us part. I just never expected it to happen so soon."

Michaela shivered in agreement despite the warm room. His words rang far too true. How many times had she felt the same way about Ethen? She had always imagined them growing old together, surrounded by their children and grandchildren. But that would never happen.

Eric ran his thumbs around the edge of his mug. "We moved out here wanting something we could call our own. Lots of people went out west to California to look for gold, but we decided to stay a bit closer to home.

"Rebecca came right away, and every few years there was a little one arriving. Susanna loved babies. She said she always wanted to have a baby in the house because they added so much joy. The sad thing is that what brought her joy is also what brought me and the children so much pain." He sobered. "She died giving birth to Ruby."

Michaela took another sip of her coffee, feeling the depth of his pain from her own experience. "I know you miss her tremendously."

"I do. I'm reminded of what we made together every day, and yet, over the years, the pain has lessened, to a degree anyway."

Michaela leaned back in her chair and studied the man sitting across from her. Here was someone who understood the pain of losing a spouse. On the outside he seemed to have found a measure of peace over the event. The familiar question returned. How long would it take for her pain of losing Ethen and Leah to lessen?

"I remember when Daniel and Emma went back East to be with you." His gaze softened. "Our church prayed for you."

"Thank you so much." She turned and watched the orange and yellow flames of the fire, reminding her of the flames that had taken the lives of her family and Anna's parents. "I'm sorry, it's just that. . ."

"You don't have to explain. I understand." He seemed to sense her need for them to change the subject. "Tell me about Boston. I understand you taught piano there."

An hour later, Michaela glanced at her watch, surprised they'd talked so long.

She pushed aside the partial cup of coffee that had long since grown cold. "I really need to go. I told Daniel and Emma I wouldn't be long."

Eric placed a few coins on the table, then pushed back his

chair. "I'm sorry to have kept you so long."

"Not at all. I've thoroughly enjoyed myself."

He helped her put on her coat before they walked toward the front door. "Rebecca's excited you're helping her plan Thanksgiving dinner."

"I'm looking forward to it. Hopefully Emma will feel up to coming."

A cold wind greeted them as they stepped outside the hotel restaurant. Michaela pulled her long coat closer.

"She had to grow up so fast when her mother died, and I've always felt guilty about that," he confessed. "The truth is, now she really has grown up."

Michaela untied Honey from the post and turned to Eric. "She came to talk to me the other day. I hope you don't mind."

Eric's brow lowered, and Michaela wondered if she'd made a mistake in talking to Rebecca.

"I'm sorry if I overstepped my bounds—"

"No, please don't feel that way. It's just that. . ." He shoved his hands in his coat pockets and shook his head. "It's hard raising a family alone. Rebecca was so angry with me, but I have to do what I think is best."

"And she knows that, trust me. You're a lucky man to have such a wonderful family."

He grasped her hand and helped her into the saddle. Slowly, she pulled away, still feeling the warmth from his touch. She felt the wind whip around her and shivered, wondering if she would ever find the courage to open up her heart and love again.

nine

The sun shone Thanksgiving Day, and though a thin layer of snow still covered the ground outside, the Johnson house stayed warm from the fire in the living room. The day before, after preparing the turkey, Michaela had helped Rebecca make three pumpkin pies and what Michaela had been told was Eric's favorite, Marlborough pudding, a traditional dish made from stewed apples, sugar, and nutmeg that was baked in a piecrust. Today, they worked to finish the rest of the special meal before the guests arrived.

"I can't believe you talked my father into letting me invite Jake's family over for Thanksgiving dinner, Mrs. Macintosh." Rebecca looked up from the onion she was chopping and smiled. "Thank you."

"You're welcome." Michaela finished peeling the last potato that she'd later mash and serve with cream and butter. "Didn't I tell you that you just needed to let your father get used to the idea?"

Starting on another onion, Rebecca nodded. "He still hasn't agreed to let Jake call on me, but at least maybe this way he'll get to know him better."

"Exactly."

Rebecca set her knife down on the counter and leaned forward. "Have you ever thought about letting someone court you again, Mrs. Macintosh? You'd be good for my father."

Michaela's eyes widened in surprise as she poured the

potatoes into the boiling water. Surely Rebecca wasn't trying to play matchmaker. "Not really. I—"

Her answer was interrupted as Eric walked into the kitchen. All she could do was pray he hadn't caught the last of their conversation. Yes, she had thought about courting again, but with Philip, not Eric Johnson.

"How long until supper, ladies?" Eric leaned over and kissed his daughter on the top of her head. "I understand that a certain young man is joining us."

A soft blush crossed Rebecca's face as she began vigorously chopping one of the onions. "Everyone should arrive about four o'clock."

"Good." Eric walked near to where Michaela was working on the potatoes and picked up a spoon. "That will give me plenty of time to talk to Jake."

Rebecca's knife clattered against the counter. "Father, promise me you'll be extra nice to him."

Eric didn't answer but instead began peeking under several of the covered dishes. "Did you make any Marlborough pudding?"

Rebecca nodded. "It's already finished."

Spoon in hand, Eric stopped when he found the dessert.

"All right, Eric Johnson." Michaela set her hands firmly against her hips. "You're about to be in trouble with both of us."

His mouth curved into a smile. "Someone's got to sample the food."

Michaela shook her head like a stern schoolteacher. "No sampling until dinner, and promise your daughter you won't do anything to embarrass her."

"Of course I won't." Eric winked at his daughter, then left the room.

Rebecca turned to Michaela. "You don't really think he'd do anything to embarrass me, do you?"

"He's your father, Rebecca. He loves you. He's probably just as anxious as you are." Michaela added some salt to the boiling potatoes. "This is new territory for both of you, and you're going to have the normal ups and downs in your relationship with your father, but he would never hurt you on purpose."

Rebecca nodded. "I know you're right. I'm just so nervous about today. Don't you think Jake's handsome?"

Michaela laughed as Rebecca proceeded to tell her how his eyes were the clearest blue she'd ever seen and how, being interested in politics, he knew absolutely everything about Governor Long. Michaela listened intently to the young girl's stories about Jake and remembered similar conversations shared with Aunt Clara about Ethen. It was good to feel needed. For the first time in a long time, Michaela felt truly happy.

ta

Two hours later, the three families finished the meal. The entire day had been a success. Even Emma had felt up to coming to the celebration.

Michaela helped Rebecca serve the pumpkin pies and Marlborough pudding.

"This looks fantastic." Eric smiled at his daughter and took the plate Rebecca offered him that held a thick slice of each dessert.

Michaela served Jake and smiled. True to his word, Eric had helped put the young man at ease and seemed to take today as an opportunity to get to know him better. It was obvious by the smile that hadn't left Rebecca's face that she was pleased with the way the afternoon was turning out.

A fork clattered against the china plate. Perplexed, Michaela watched Adam gulp down his glass of water.

She eyed her piece of pumpkin pie, wondering if something could be wrong with the dessert, but it looked perfect. She sampled a bit of the pie and froze. Instead of the sweet pumpkin flavor she'd expected, it tasted as if she'd just taken a spoonful of salt.

"What's wrong?" Rebecca noticed the startled looks on everyone's faces.

"It's the pumpkin pie." Michaela felt a wave of nausea wash over her. This dinner meant so much to Rebecca.

Rebecca took a bite, then promptly spat it out. "What happened?" She sat motionless in her chair beside the one person she'd tried to impress all day.

"I think you switched the sugar for salt, sweetheart." Eric's sympathetic smile didn't faze Rebecca.

"I couldn't have. I. . ."

A quiet giggle came from the other side of the table. Sarah sat hunched down in her chair, her hands across her mouth. "I'm sorry, it's just—"

"This is not funny, Sarah," Eric warned her.

Michaela stood from the table and began gathering up the plates of uneaten pie. Jake sent Rebecca a sympathetic glance but seemed to be at odds at how to remedy the situation. Sarah's giggles continued despite the sharp look from her father.

Eric crossed his arms and leaned toward his middle daughter, who sat across from him. "Sarah Phoebe Johnson, if you know anything about the extra salt in your sister's pie, you'd better tell me right now."

Sarah's giggles stopped.

"Sarah. . ."

She bit her lip and looked at her father out of the corner of her eye. Michaela set the stack of dishes at the edge of the table, wondering what she should do. Rebecca had spent days planning this meal, and if Sarah had something to do with the ruined pie, she knew it would crush Rebecca.

"I. . ." Sarah stifled another laugh.

"You still think this is funny?" Eric kept his voice low, but it was laced with anger.

"Yes—no." Sarah's gaze dropped to the floor. "I switched the sugar for the salt in the filling when Rebecca wasn't looking yesterday. She was so busy, she didn't even notice what I did. It was supposed to be funny."

Rebecca let out a sob, then fled from the room. Eric stood and threw his napkin on the table. Sarah slid down farther in her chair.

"Eric." Michaela took a few steps toward him until they were only inches apart. She knew she shouldn't interfere, but Rebecca was the one who needed her father right now. "Let me talk to Sarah. Go find Rebecca. She needs you now."

Eric nodded and stepped out the front door to find his daughter.

"I'll get the dishes." Mrs. Markham stood to finish clearing the table, while Michaela nodded at Sarah to follow her up to the girl's room.

Sitting across from her on the bed, Michaela watched as Sarah chewed on her thumbnail. "I remember one summer when I was eleven years old. It was the worst summer I'd ever had. I'd been sick a lot and wasn't allowed to go outside and play most of the time. Then, in late August, we celebrated my brother's eighteenth birthday. He would be leaving soon to go to school, and my parents wanted the day to be extra special. I was in charge of serving the punch at the party. The more they planned, the more jealous I got. They'd never thrown a party like that for me, so I decided to do something so no one would forget I was around."

Sarah leaned forward. "What did you do?"

"Attempting to make it look like an accident, I dumped the punch off the table and onto my mother's beige carpet."

"Guess your parents didn't think that was funny, either."

"No, they didn't." Michaela prayed for the right words. "Truth was, I loved my brother a lot, and I didn't like the changes that were taking place. I knew he would be leaving, and I didn't want him to go."

Sarah shook her head. "Sometimes it seems like everything's changing."

"What are you really afraid of, Sarah?"

She was still for a moment. "If Rebecca gets married, things will never be the same again."

Michaela smiled and patted Sarah gently on her arm. "You're right. Things won't ever be the same again. But it also means that before you know it, some handsome boy will be calling on you."

Sarah groaned, but it was obvious she wasn't totally displeased with the idea. "I suppose I would hate it if Ruby or one of the boys did something like that to me."

"I think you're exactly right." Michaela smiled. "Besides that, you'd have to come up with a lot better idea to chase Rebecca's beaus away, because I don't think some extra salt in the pie would deter very many of them."

Sarah dropped her gaze. "It was awful, wasn't it?"

Michaela nodded in agreement. "I think you have a few

people you need to talk to, starting with your sister."

❧

Eric hurried out of the house and into the barn. Climbing up the sturdy ladder to the loft, he found Rebecca sitting on a bale of hay with tears silently streaming down her face.

"How'd you know I'd be here?" Rebecca looked up at him. The hurt in her eyes broke his heart.

"You told me one time this was your favorite place to think."

Eric rubbed his hands together, more from nerves than the cold wind that blew through the cracks in the walls. Sitting down beside her, he prayed for wisdom. "I'm sorry about what happened."

"Why would Sarah do something like that?" Rebecca wiped her cheeks with the backs of her hands and shook her head. "I know it's silly to care about a bunch of stupid pies, but—"

"Your feelings aren't silly." Eric took his daughter's hands in his. "Today was important for you. I know that."

Rebecca looked up at him; her gaze seemed to plead with him to understand. "I really care about Jake. I know you're not ready for me to grow up, but I'm seventeen. You married Mother when she was barely eighteen."

Eric let out a soft laugh at the truth behind her words. How come his own daughter seemed so much younger than he and Susanna had been when they married? The truth was, his daughter was just as mature and responsible as he had ever been at eighteen. He just didn't want to admit it.

"I never thought I'd have to go through all of this alone, Rebecca." It was times like this when he missed Susanna the most. Missed her support and encouragement. Her wisdom. A man wasn't meant to raise six children alone. For the first time in a long time, he felt the cold reality of being a widower.

Eric turned and placed both of his hands on her shoulders. "Rebecca Margaret Johnson, you are my firstborn, and I love you unconditionally. I know that I could never take the place of your mother in raising you. There are simply too many emotions you feel that, as a man, I can't understand. But what I do know is that you and I are going to get through this together. Just give me some time to get used to the idea of another man caring for you."

Rebecca cocked her head and lowered her brows in question. "Does that mean you'll let Jake court me?"

"I didn't say that." He saw the disappointment in her eyes. It was time, and he knew it. "Though I suppose I should consider it. Especially if it means I'll get more dinners like tonight's."

Rebecca's face lit up. "Do you mean it? Will you talk to him?"

Eric nodded, realizing that in agreeing to Rebecca's request, he was letting go of her. Before he knew it, he'd be walking his daughter down the aisle, and she'd leave his home to live with someone else. He'd known the day would come, but he wasn't ready yet.

"I suppose this means Jake will be coming around a bit more?"

"You like him, don't you?"

He had to admit the truth, even though he doubted he would ever meet someone good enough for his daughter. "He's a fine young man."

"What about you?" Rebecca reached out and straightened the collar of his shirt.

He raised his brow in question. "What about me?"

"Have you thought about courting again?"

Eric leaned back, pushing the palms of his hands against his thighs. Had Rebecca noticed his interest in Michaela? "You think we need a woman in our lives?"

"After tonight?" She flashed him a broad smile. "Yes."

He combed his fingers through his hair. "Courting would mean a lot of changes for us. We're used to doing things on our own. You'd have to stay with the children while I'm out eating at a restaurant or taking her out on a picnic."

Eric liked the idea but had worried about his children's reactions. He had thoroughly enjoyed having coffee with Michaela earlier this week. In fact, since Susanna's death, he hadn't felt as comfortable talking with another woman as he did with Michaela.

Rebecca folded her arms across her chest and smiled again. "Of course, it would have to be the right person."

"Are you thinking about anyone in particular?"

Rebecca nodded, and he caught the gleam in her eye. "There is one person I've thought for quite a while now would be perfect for you. Michaela Macintosh."

~

Michaela handed Mrs. Markham the last dish to dry, then wiped down the long counter. She'd found the woman's company pleasant but couldn't keep her mind off Eric and the conversation he was having with Rebecca. Silently, she prayed that God would give him the wisdom he would need, not only for tonight, but in the weeks and months to come.

Eric stepped into the kitchen and addressed Michaela. "Can we talk?"

Michaela nodded at Eric's request and followed him outside onto the front porch, where they could have a semblance of privacy. He leaned against the porch rail and looked at her, his brow furrowed into deep creases. Michaela's stomach constricted. This time she had overstepped her boundaries. She never should have suggested talking to Sarah. It wasn't her place. It was Eric's.

"Eric, I need to apologize—"

"Wait, please." He held up his hand in protest. "I need to say this."

Michaela swallowed hard and let her gaze sweep across the terrain, now a maze of shadows in the fading sunlight. Whatever he had to say, she deserved it.

Eric cleared his throat. "When you first offered to teach piano to the children, I was thrilled to have them gain that experience. I have slowly had to realize that there are many things I simply can't do as their father. I struggle with talking to Rebecca about becoming a woman and to Sarah about how to dress like a lady. A man wasn't meant to be both father and mother to his children. We need someone like you in our lives."

Michaela's hands clenched the rail. Surely he wasn't planning to propose some kind of marriage of convenience. Eric took a step toward her. "I just wanted to thank you for being a friend to my children. I know I haven't always put you in an easy position, but you've been there for them when they needed you, and I appreciate that."

Michaela felt the heat rise to her face, thankful she hadn't made a fool of herself by saying something she'd regret later. If all he was saying was thank you. . .

She coughed softly. "God has blessed you with six marvelous children, and I've enjoyed the short time I've been able to spend with them. However, I by no means want to overstep my bounds—"

"You haven't, trust me. In fact, I was afraid you might feel that way, and I wanted to assure you that you hadn't."

Sarah stepped out of the house and onto the porch, a somber expression on her face. Michaela felt sure it would be awhile before Sarah attempted another stunt like she'd pulled today.

Sarah stood in front of her father, her hands fidgeting at her sides. "I apologized to Rebecca and the others, and I want you to know how truly sorry I am."

Eric gathered his daughter into his arms, and Michaela slipped back into the house to let them be alone.

She found Emma lying on the couch in the parlor. "Are you all right?"

"Just resting. It's been a long day, but I didn't want Daniel to have to leave early. I believe he and Mr. Markham are caught up in a game of chess."

"I think everyone has had a nice day today."

"I noticed you and Eric spending a lot of time together today." Emma propped herself up on her elbow. "Do you simply enjoy his company, or could it be something else?"

"Eric's a good friend and nothing else." Michaela immediately regretted her sharp tone. "I'm sorry, Emma. It has been a long day, and I'm tired."

Michaela rubbed her temples with her fingertips. She needed to take a step back. Her emotions were becoming far too entwined in the lives of this family. She'd be leaving in a few weeks, and then what? Maybe if she went riding for a bit, she could clear her head.

"Since I rode Honey out here, I think I'll go on home. If I'm not there by the time you get back, I'll be there shortly."

Emma pulled her shawl across her shoulders. "I need to get home soon as well. Don't stay out too long. It will be dark soon."

A crisp, chilly breeze played with the loose wisps of hair peeking out of Michaela's hood as she left the Johnson farm. Squinting against the brightness of the setting sun, she took in a deep breath of the frosty air.

She touched her skirt pocket and felt the crackling of paper under the material. She had received another letter from Philip yesterday. Anna had celebrated her sixth birthday, and he and Caroline had spent part of the day with her, giving her the tea set Michaela sent and a wooden pony Philip had carved.

The most important news had followed. The couple planning to adopt Anna had changed their minds and decided to adopt only a boy.

The answer seemed so clear. Wasn't Philip everything she could want in a man? He was a strong Christian with high moral standards who treated her with respect and one who would cherish and take care of her.

Michaela sighed, remembering how many times Daniel and Emma had each tried their hand at arousing her interest in Eric. He might be a handsome, eligible bachelor, but that didn't mean he was the one for her.

Michaela pulled gently on the reins and brought Honey to a stop. She looked toward the west, where the yellow and red of the sunset spread across the sky like a bucket of spilled paint. Philip had asked her to marry him, and she was going to accept.

Michaela turned Honey and headed toward the farm, ready to tell Daniel and Emma her decision. She'd kept her feelings for Philip quiet for too long. It was time to move forward with her life.

After bedding Honey down for the night, Michaela hurried

into the house, where she found Daniel and Emma sitting in the parlor. A smile played across Michaela's lips.

"Eric proposed?" Daniel set down the book he was reading and looked up at Michaela with a sly grin across his face.

Michaela put her hands on her hips and gave her brother an exasperated look. "No, but it does have to do with proposals. I've made a decision. I'm going to marry Philip."

Emma leaned forward on the sofa. "I knew his feelings for you were strong, but if we'd realized you shared his feelings, we never would have teased you about Eric. It's just that you've rarely spoken of Philip."

"I know." Michaela sat on the edge of the mahogany armchair across from them. "I may not have talked about him much, but in these past couple of months, I've been forced to think about where I want my life to go. Marrying Philip is what I want. He's kind, compassionate, and he loves me unconditionally."

"You don't have to convince us. As long as you are happy, then we're happy for you." Daniel stood and pulled her to her feet, wrapping his arms around her. "Philip's a good man, and I know he'll make you very happy."

"Why don't you send him a telegram and tell him?" Emma suggested, drawing her legs up beneath her. "You know he'll be elated."

"I wish I could tell him myself." Michaela felt the ache of homesickness increase for a moment, but she knew her place was here for now. Philip would wait for her, of that she had no doubt. And Anna would be there as well. A wave of peace washed over her. "I'll go into town tomorrow."

After the baby came, she would go home to Boston, where she belonged.

ten

Sarah tried the scale for the tenth time.

"Have you been practicing?" Michaela asked.

"Well. . ."

"Sarah, if you don't practice, I can't teach you anything. You have to practice."

"The other kids are always on the piano."

Michaela felt her patience waning. "I happen to know that your father worked out a time schedule so each of you have at least thirty minutes a day."

"Yes, but. . ."

"Sarah, you have to practice."

"Then I'll be able to play as good as you?"

Michaela decided to use a new approach. "Can I tell you a secret?"

Sarah leaned forward, her face lit with a grin.

"God has gifted you with a talent in music that far exceeds my own. Not only do you have a beautiful voice, but you have talent to play the piano as well."

Sarah pulled back, looking doubtful at Michaela's assessment. "Do you really think so?"

Michaela nodded. "I know it's true. But even someone as talented as you are has to practice."

Someone yelled outside, and Michaela and Sarah hurried to the window. Eric and the boys were running in circles around the front yard, chasing the chickens.

115

"The chickens are loose!" Ruby ran outside, whooping in delight.

Michaela steered Sarah back to the piano. "We'd better get back to our lesson."

Fifteen minutes later, the front door slammed. Eric stomped into the house, followed by the boys.

"Someone left the gate open to the chicken coop." Eric flopped down in a chair and started taking off his boots. "Do you know how difficult it is to catch over thirty chickens?"

"I saw how difficult it is." Michaela stifled a laugh.

Eric didn't smile. "Does anyone know who left the gate to the chicken coop open?"

By now all the children had gathered in the room, but Eric's focus was on Sarah and Ruby. If Michaela remembered correctly, it was their responsibility to gather the eggs each day and feed the chickens.

"I'm sure we shut the gate." Sarah nudged Ruby with her elbow.

"Did you latch it?" Eric leaned forward and rested his elbows against his thighs.

The girls looked at each other and squirmed in their chairs.

"The animals are part of our livelihood." Eric pulled off his other boot and set it beside him. "You may think it's humorous to watch your father run circles around a bunch of squawking chickens, but I don't."

Several of the children let out quiet chuckles. Michaela bit her lip, trying not to laugh. Eric's gaze swept the room, then stopped at Michaela.

"Looks like we're even," she said with a grin.

Eric raised his brows in question.

"Have you forgotten the day I fell in the mud? I seem to

recall at least one person who couldn't keep a straight face."

The sides of Eric's mouth slowly curled into a grin as he shrugged in defeat. He turned to Ruby and Sarah. "I guess I owe you an apology. I had a frustrating morning in town, and I shouldn't take it out on you. I'm sorry."

The girls ran to give their father a hug, and Eric kept an arm wrapped around each of them. "But that doesn't excuse the fact that you weren't careful. From now on, please make sure you latch the gate so this doesn't happen again."

Two heads bobbed in unison.

Eric turned to his oldest daughter. "How long until dinner, Rebecca?"

"Ten minutes."

"Good, because I, for one, worked up quite an appetite."

"Can Mrs. Macintosh join us for dinner, Father?" Sarah asked.

"You'll have to ask her."

"Will you stay?" Ruby ran and jumped into Michaela's lap.

Michaela pulled the young girl close and nuzzled her chin against the top of her head, breathing in the familiar scent of lavender. "How could I refuse? Daniel and Emma's dinner's on the stove, and I've been wanting some more of Rebecca's excellent cooking."

Rebecca blushed and headed into the kitchen.

Eric carried his boots toward the front door. "Everyone needs to get washed up."

Michaela went into the kitchen to help Rebecca with dinner. "What can I do to help?"

"The bread still needs to be sliced."

Michaela cut the fresh loaf of bread into thick pieces while the children began to trickle in and take their places at the table.

"Smells delicious." Eric entered the room and kissed his oldest daughter on her forehead. "Nothing like a roast with vegetables."

After Michaela finished helping Rebecca serve the meal, Eric pulled back the empty chair beside him and motioned for her to sit. "As our guest, you're working too hard, Michaela."

Michaela slid into the chair and glanced around the long table at the children who had, in such a short time, become an integral part of her life. Eric led the family in a prayer, which was followed by echoes of "amen" around the table.

"This meal is wonderful, Rebecca." Eric put a large spoonful of vegetables on his plate.

Rebecca smiled, obviously pleased with her father's compliment. "Sarah and Ruby planned to ask you to stay for dinner, Mrs. Macintosh, so I tried to fix something extra special."

"I'm honored to be here." Michaela spread homemade jam over a thick slice of bread. Besides the roast and bread, there were mashed potatoes, green beans, and apple cobbler for dessert.

Michaela took another bite of her roast and listened to the children's laughter as they shared what had happened throughout the school week. The animated conversation centered on school and the upcoming Christmas holiday, and she found herself enjoying the lively banter between Eric and his children.

After a short lull in the conversation, Eric turned to Michaela. "I've never asked you what you think of our house."

She waved her hand in the air. "It's beautiful. The girls gave me a tour a few weeks ago. They told me you built it yourself."

Eric set his fork on his plate and chuckled. "It's become

one of those never-ending projects. We started off small, but with each child, we needed a bit more room and thus added on every few years."

"Tell us about Boston." Sarah leaned forward expectantly.

Michaela wiped the corners of her mouth with a napkin, then set the cloth in her lap. "My aunt and I live on the outskirts of the city, not far from the ocean."

Sarah's eyes widened. "I've never seen the ocean! What's it like?"

Michaela smiled at Sarah's innocent wonder. "It's hard to describe, it's so vast. As far as you can see, the blues and greens of the ocean spread out before you—wave after wave making its way toward the shore."

"What about the city?" Samuel spoke for the first time.

"Boston is full of people, businesses, and crowded streets. There are so many stores and restaurants, you can easily get lost if you don't know your way around. There are also museums, art galleries, and a university."

"Sounds wonderful." Samuel squirmed in his chair, excitement mounting in his voice. "Someday I want to go back East for school."

"Samuel wants to be a doctor," Eric said, the pride obvious in his voice.

"I'm sure you'll make a fine doctor."

"What do you do in Boston?" Ruby asked.

Michaela played with the linen napkin in her hands. "Before my husband died, I worked with him. He and his brother owned a cabinetmaking shop."

"Is it a big factory?" Samuel asked.

Michaela nodded. "There are about a dozen men who work there, plus a showroom where they sell the furniture. My job was to keep up the books."

"But you don't do that anymore?" Sarah asked.

Michaela shook her head. "Lately I've been teaching piano lessons. It's something I've always wanted to do."

"And now you teach us." Ruby grinned and turned to whisper something in Sarah's ear.

"Girls," Eric said, "if there is something you need to say, say it so the rest of us can hear you."

They giggled, then looked at Michaela.

"Girls. . . ," their father prompted again.

"We were wondering," Sarah began. "Could we have a sing-along this afternoon?"

"Yes." Ruby's head bobbed up and down. "You could play the piano and the rest of us could sing."

"That would be fun." Rebecca stood and began clearing the dishes.

"Only if Michaela agrees." Eric turned to her, and by his expression, he seemed pleased with the idea. "We haven't done that for quite a long time."

"Sounds like fun." Michaela smiled but inwardly fought a wave of sadness. Sitting at the table with Eric and his children, she suddenly realized how familiar her presence in this house had become—and how at ease she felt. She wouldn't be here to be a part of Rebecca's courtship or Adam's upcoming graduation. She swallowed hard. And then there was Eric.

Eric's voice stopped her thoughts from wandering to a place she was afraid to go. "I need all of you to help Rebecca clean up the kitchen. I need to take care of something outside, then I'll be in."

Michaela joined in the familiar task of drying dishes. Sarah and Matt put them in their right places, and before long the kitchen was in order, ready for the next meal. As soon as they were done, Sarah and Ruby begged to be allowed to show Michaela the new litter of puppies in the barn.

"Pa's not back yet," Sarah pleaded. "Can we, please?"

Rebecca nodded her head. "Just don't be long."

Michaela followed the girls outside to the barn, where she was introduced to Sarah's brood of animals.

"She's adorable." Michaela took the puppy Ruby handed her and was greeted with a face full of wet kisses. The puppy couldn't have been more than a few weeks old.

"And this is Red," Ruby announced, petting an older dog.

Michaela was then introduced to five cats, Pinky the pig, and Beaker, Sarah's favorite chicken. She was campaigning so it wouldn't end up on the dinner table.

After a few minutes, they stepped back outside and into the bright sunshine, with Red still jumping and barking around them.

On the way back to the house, Sarah pointed to their garden, freshly tilled for the winter months.

"The garden is our job." Ruby puckered up her nose.

"We have to make sure there are no weeds," Sarah added.

"Running a farm takes a lot of work," Michaela said to the girls.

"Most of the time it's fun," Sarah jabbered. "There's harvesttime when all the people in the area get together for a big celebration, swimming in the summer, horseback riding, and best of all, Christmas is coming."

"Christmas was always one of my favorite times of the year." Michaela felt a rush of emotion. "I always loved the lights and the trees decorated so beautifully. My mother and I used to make gingerbread men and frosted sugar cookies."

Ruby stopped and looked up into Michaela's eyes. "If you like Christmas, then why does your face look so sad?"

Michaela took a deep breath, wishing her feelings weren't so transparent. She ruffled Ruby's hair. "I had a little girl who would have been about your age. She and her daddy died in a fire on Christmas Eve."

Ruby's eyes narrowed. "Then this Christmas, maybe we can help make you happy again."

Michaela smiled as each of the girls took one of her hands, seemingly trying to comfort her.

"Our mother died when I was born," Ruby said as the three of them slowly walked back to the house together. A gentle wind blew, rustling the leaves in the trees. "Father's always sad on my birthday."

"I know she loved you." Michaela knelt down and faced Ruby. "For nine months, she carried you inside of her and dreamed about what you would look like, what you would become someday."

"Really?"

"Really."

They were silent for a moment until Sarah spoke again. "We'd better go back to the house. I just saw Father go inside. It's time for the sing-along."

❧

Michaela ran her limber fingers across the keys, enjoying a final chorus. Her high soprano voice and Eric's deep bass blended with the children's voices, which rang with energy and enthusiasm. Even the boys, who hadn't seemed excited about the idea, looked as if they were enjoying the singing.

"It's going to be dark before long." Eric slapped his hands against his thighs and pulled Ruby against his side. "This has been wonderful, Michaela. Thank you."

There were groans of protest from the children until they saw their father's stern look, reminding them he meant what he said. "I'll be happy to take you home, Michaela."

"You don't have to do that." Michaela stretched out her fingers, then tilted her head from side to side to loosen some of the muscles in her neck.

"It's no problem at all." Eric grabbed his coat from the hook beside the door. "Honey can follow behind the wagon."

"All right then." Michaela put on her coat and said good-bye to the children before following him outside.

"It's beautiful out tonight." Sitting next to Eric in the wagon, Michaela watched as the last sliver of sun sank into the horizon. "I remember sunrises with my grandfather. We would sit on one of the rocks along the beach until the sun made its appearance over the ocean."

"I miss the ocean." There was a wistful tone to Eric's voice. "It used to be one of my favorite places. Someday I want to take the children to the coast and show them the ocean."

"They'd love that." Michaela's spirits brightened at the idea. "Come to Boston. I'll be there and can show them around."

They rode in silence for a moment as a mass of stars took their places with the full moon in the sky.

After a few minutes, Eric spoke. "How long do you plan to stay in Cranton?"

"I'll go back to Boston after the baby is born and Emma's back on her feet. Probably just a few more weeks now." The slight tug of disappointment returned.

"What do you want to do when you go back?"

"I'll continue teaching piano for a while—"

He shook his head. "That's not what I mean."

She turned and looked at him, her brows raised in question. "What do you mean?"

"I know it's really none of my business, but while you seem so good at taking care of others, I wondered what your dreams are."

It was something she'd never thought about. Two years ago, she'd known exactly what she wanted. She loved being a mother and a wife. But all of that had changed. How could she even begin to understand what she wanted out of life?

When she didn't answer, Eric gently slapped the reins, his gaze seemingly lost in the distant horizon. "After my wife died, I felt so out of control. All my time and energy went into working the farm and caring for the children—until finally I realized if I didn't take care of myself, both emotionally and spiritually, I wouldn't be able to do anything after a while. All I want to say is that it's all right to think about what your own needs are."

The words seemed to pierce straight through her soul. She regularly turned to God, full of requests and needs, but wasn't there supposed to be so much more to her relationship with her heavenly Father? When was the last time she'd studied her Bible? What about times of worship and adoration? She suddenly realized how empty she was spiritually. Could the fact that she'd been neglecting her relationship with God be the reason she felt both spiritually and emotionally drained? It seemed so simple, but somehow she'd missed it.

" 'O come, let us worship and bow down: let us kneel before the Lord our maker.' " Michaela spoke the words from the Bible aloud, barely more than a whisper.

Eric must have heard her quiet voice. "One of David's psalms?"

Michaela nodded and clasped her hands in front of her. "You know, you're right. I've been so busy trying to stay busy, it seems my prayers have become nothing more than one-sided requests when I'm hurting or needing something. I can't remember the last time my heart was full of praise and worship."

Eric slowed the horses as they came to the top of a slight ridge and started down the other side. "That's an essential part of our relationship with Christ and in our healing."

Michaela unfolded her hands and played with the folds of her skirt. A light snow had begun to fall. She watched a flake land on the material, then slowly melt. "It's still so hard. I want to forget the past, and I'm good at staying busy so there isn't time to think. Losing Ethen and Leah was the hardest thing that ever happened to me."

"Psalm 47 says, 'He healeth the broken in heart, and bindeth up their wounds.'"

Daniel and Emma's frame house appeared in the distance. In the past few months, it had become a haven of safety for her, but she had neglected to let Christ be her true refuge. Eric had reminded her of something she'd ignored in her life, and she knew she couldn't just leave it at that.

Eric stopped the horses in front of the house. "I really enjoyed spending the afternoon with you."

"Thank you for such a wonderful afternoon, Eric."

Eric jumped down from the wagon and hurried to the other side, where he helped Michaela down. As her foot hit the ground, she lost her balance and fell against Eric's chest. She looked up into his eyes, and before she knew what was happening, his lips met hers.

For a moment, she felt herself responding.

"No!" She pushed herself away, still feeling the burning sensation on her lips.

"I'm sorry." Eric looked down at her. "I didn't plan to kiss you, Michaela. It just seemed so natural."

"It's not that; it's just. . ."

Questions flashed through her mind as she tried to stop the panic rising in her throat. What about Philip? She started to slowly back away from Eric.

"Wait, Michaela." Eric gently brushed a snowflake off the end of her nose. "Tell me the truth, Michaela. Is it just me, or do you feel something as well?"

Michaela took a deep breath, trying desperately to make sense out of her jumbled emotions. She knew she felt a strong physical attraction to Eric, but was there something more? Something deeper?

No! I'm going home to Philip.

"Is there someone back in Boston?" He glanced down at his boots. Swallowing hard, he looked off to one side, clenching his jaw and waiting for her response.

"No. . .Yes!" Michaela's eyes were wide with confusion as she looked at Eric. "I'm sorry. I wasn't expecting this."

"Neither was I."

"There is. . ." *I have to tell him the truth. I have to tell him about Philip.*

Michaela searched for the right words, but something held her back. Her mind spun out of control. She couldn't think clearly. She had to get inside the house.

"Maybe I'm wrong." Eric drew a deep breath. "I thought there was something between us. I apologize. It just all seemed so real today with you and the kids, and the ride home. Then when I kissed you. . ."

"I'm sorry." Michaela wiped away a tear with the back of her hand, turned around, and ran toward the house.

Daniel and Emma were sitting on the sofa and talking when Michaela burst into the parlor. "Daniel, would you please put Honey into her stall?" Michaela hurried into her room and threw herself on the bed.

What was the matter with her? How could she have reacted this way over a kiss? And more importantly, why hadn't she told Eric the truth?

If deciding to marry Philip was supposed to simplify her life, why did things suddenly seem so complicated? Marrying Philip was the right decision. But if that were true, why had Eric's kiss turned her heart, and maybe her life, upside down?

❧

Eric dug the pitchfork into the loose hay, trying to get his mind off Michaela—something he hadn't been able to do for the past two hours. He wiped the sweat from his forehead with his sleeve and sighed.

Michaela Macintosh.

She had captivated him from the moment he first laid eyes on her. These last few weeks, he found himself thinking more and more about this woman who had come into his life. He loved the way she worked with the children and her willingness to teach them piano.

She was beautiful, too. He had found himself watching her and wondered if she noticed. He loved how she constantly pushed back the stray lock of hair that always fell in her eyes and how her eyes crinkled when she laughed. When he accidentally brushed next to her, her skin was soft against his arms, and he couldn't help wondering what it would be like to hold her.

Then tonight, when he kissed her, he realized he loved her. He had known for a long time now that he missed her when she was gone, and when they were together, he couldn't keep his eyes off of her. Yes, he knew now that he loved her, but how could he have been so wrong about her feelings toward him?

Eric scooped up another mound of hay and added it to the pile. He had begun to think she was the one God had brought into his life to make him whole again—a second chance at love. He was lonely and knew he wanted to marry again, but it had to be someone who loved the children and whom the children loved as well. After today, it had all seemed so clear. How could he have been so wrong?

The barn door creaked open, and Rebecca stepped into the light of the lantern.

"Rebecca." Eric leaned against the pitchfork. "Is something wrong?"

She shook her head and walked toward him, pulling her coat closer around her. "No, I saw the light and thought you must be home. What are you doing?"

He followed her gaze to the two piles of hay. He'd worked for an hour and done nothing more than move the pile a few feet to the right. He shook his head and ran his fingers through his hair. "I couldn't sleep."

Rebecca stifled a yawn and sat down on a packed bale of hay. "What happened with Mrs. Macintosh?"

Eric closed his eyes briefly, cringing inwardly at the memory. "I kissed her."

Shadows dancing across Rebecca's face revealed a smile. "That's wonderful."

He shook his head and set the tool against the wall before coming to sit beside her. "It was supposed to be."

"I don't understand."

Eric leaned back against the barn wall and sighed. "I thought you were the one who was supposed to come to me about relationships."

"Talking helps. That's what you've always told me."

Eric closed his eyes again, but all he could see was Michaela standing in front of him. "I don't know, Rebecca. I must have totally misread her."

"I'm sorry. I, well, all of us kids really like her." She reached out and took his hand. "I just want you to be happy, Father."

Eric squeezed his daughter's hand, then stood and picked up the pitchfork again. "Go on to bed. I'll be in later."

He watched as his daughter slipped out of the barn and headed toward the house. He'd allowed her to shoulder far more responsibility than a young woman should have to deal with. All this time he'd thought he'd been handling things fine without a wife, but instead, he'd unknowingly placed a large burden on his daughter.

He needed Michaela. His family needed Michaela. And if he was right, Michaela needed them. If she could just find a way to let go of the past, then maybe, just maybe, she'd be able to take another chance at love—with him.

eleven

Michaela rose early the next morning, after a restless night. She would see Eric at church today and dreaded facing him after last night's scene. What a fool she had been. Why hadn't she just told him about Philip?

Needing to talk to someone, Michaela fixed a breakfast tray for Emma, then knocked gently on her door.

"Good morning." Michaela entered the room. Emma sat snuggled under a thick quilt reading a book. "Are you hungry?"

"You're just in time. I'm starving." Emma set the book down and pushed her long braid off her shoulder.

Michaela placed the tray on the small table beside the bed and handed Emma the steaming plate. "I'm sure glad food doesn't turn your stomach anymore."

"Me, too, except now that I can eat, I can't get out of bed." Emma laughed and took a small bite of eggs.

"Is Daniel out working already?" Michaela walked to the window and looked out across the white snow that glistened in the morning sunlight. "His breakfast is on the stove."

"Daniel's been up for hours. I don't know how he always manages to get going so early."

Michaela rubbed her hands together, then turned to face Emma. "Can I talk to you about something?"

"Of course. What is it?"

"I spent half the night thinking and praying. I had such a nice time yesterday afternoon with Eric and the kids. We ate a delicious lunch Rebecca fixed, then had a sing-along." The knot in Michaela's stomach grew, and she paced the short side of the room. "On the way home, he brought up some things that really challenged me spiritually. Things I needed to hear."

"I'm not sure I see what the problem is." Emma took a drink of her milk before setting it back on the tray.

"He kissed me."

"Oh." Emma set her fork down and gave Michaela her full attention.

Michaela took several more broad steps across the room. "Last night I lay in bed and all I wanted to do was take the next train away from here."

"Did you tell him about Philip?"

Moving back to the side of the bed, Michaela sat beside Emma, her gaze fixed on the dark brown sheen of the hardwood floor. "That's the problem. I didn't tell him."

"You didn't tell him!" Emma's voice rose slightly. "Why not?"

Michaela stood again, knowing there could be no excuse for her behavior. She had to tell him the truth, but the very thought of telling him made her stomach turn. She didn't want him to think she'd purposely deceived him. It hadn't been that at all.

She ran her hands down the sides of her dress, wiping away the moisture. "I don't know why I didn't tell him. I keep asking myself that same question over and over. When he kissed me, I couldn't think."

"He deserves the truth, Michaela."

"I know."

Emma set her plate on the tray and pulled the covers over her swollen abdomen. "Could it be you have feelings for Eric and don't want him to know about Philip?"

Michaela inwardly winced at the question, trying to disregard any truth to the notion. "The time I've spent with Eric and his children has been wonderful, but. . ."

"And now?"

"It doesn't matter." She shook her head. "Philip loves me, and I belong in Boston with him. I'm going to marry Philip."

Michaela stood up and walked back to the window. Whatever her feelings toward Eric and his children, nothing could erase the mistake she'd made. Why hadn't she told Eric about Philip? All along there had been plenty of opportunities.

"Come and sit down." Emma patted the top of the quilt beside her and Michaela complied. "Eric's the kind of man any woman would be blessed to have for a husband, and he cares about you. I know I shouldn't say this, but be careful about closing the door unless you're sure. If you really are in love with Philip, then that's wonderful, but just make sure you're not marrying Philip because it's convenient and safe. Don't do something you'll regret later on."

Michaela fought against the wisdom of her sister-in-law's advice. "It's true that I don't love Philip the same way I loved Ethen, but I don't think I'll ever love anyone as much as Ethen. Philip loves me. We'll have a good life together."

Emma bit her lip, and it was obvious to Michaela she wanted to say more. Needing to be alone with her thoughts, Michaela stood and went to the door. "I'd better get ready for church. Do you need anything else?"

"No, but come and talk to me anytime you need to."

Michaela turned around, her hand against the doorknob. "Thank you."

☙

Michaela looked for Eric as she sat down on the pew next to

her brother. All the Johnson kids were there except Ruby, and there was no sign of Eric.

The service began, and after singing two songs, the minister stood before the congregation.

" 'If the Son therefore shall make you free, ye shall be free indeed.' " He began the morning's sermon, quoting from John 8:36.

Michaela forced herself to concentrate on the lesson, but the memory of Eric's hurt expression the night before continued to haunt her.

As soon as services were over, Michaela followed Daniel out to the wagon without getting a chance to talk to the Johnson children. He hated to leave Emma even for a short amount of time and wanted to hurry back to the house. Michaela sat silent for the first five minutes, thinking only of the words from the sermon.

"I think starting next week I'll let you ride to church alone," Daniel said as they passed the town cemetery and rode into the shadows of the covered bridge. "Emma's due date is right around the corner, and I don't want anything to happen while I'm gone."

"We can switch off until the baby's born, if you like." Michaela stared out across the landscape but saw little.

Daniel reached over and patted his sister's hand.

"You've seemed a bit. . .I don't know if depressed is right, but maybe distracted lately. I hope you're not working too hard."

"No, it's not that." Michaela decided to tell him the truth. "It's Eric."

"He's interested in you?"

Michaela grasped her Bible tightly against her chest and nodded. "I didn't realize he had feelings for me. Everyone kept hinting, but I just ignored it. I guess I should have noticed, but I didn't want to."

"I'm not surprised."

"There's more." Michaela felt another wave of guilt consume her. "I didn't tell him about Philip."

Daniel's brows rose in question. "Why not?"

"I'm still trying to understand how I feel. When Ethen and Leah died, I wanted to die, too. Sometimes I feel like my life is spinning out of control. When I decided to accept Philip's proposal, I felt like I had control over my life again." She rolled a piece of the fabric of her skirt between her forefingers. "Then today I realized the truth. God's the only One who can truly set us free from our past. I have to let Him be totally in control of my life."

" 'If the Son therefore shall make you free, ye shall be free indeed.' "

Michaela knew she was free through Christ because her past sins had been forgiven. But what did it really mean to be set free?

"In Christ we have freedom from sin." Michaela struggled to formulate her thoughts. "What about freedom from other things? The fruits of the Spirit are clear—love, joy, peace, patience, and so forth."

She let her gaze scan the horizon. "What I'm trying to say is, aren't we free from what's contrary to these fruits?" Things began to grow clear for her. "As Christians, we leave the past and our sins behind, and in turn we are to live like the Spirit. That means we give up hate, discord, sorrow, and impatience."

"You're right." Daniel tilted his head and nodded in agreement. "I've never thought about it that way."

Michaela took a deep breath and looked at her brother.

"I felt convicted today during the lesson, because I'm still carrying with me the pain, sorrow, and even guilt over Ethen's and Leah's deaths. I know God understands our pain and that the grief we go through is a part of healing, but instead of healing, I've been holding on tightly to it."

Michaela clenched her fists together in her lap. "I haven't walked with the Spirit of God, allowing Him to restore me and fill me with the joy of His presence."

The grief that had been bottled up inside her for so long began to flow down her cheeks, but Michaela's heart lit with joy. "See, God is the only One who can give me back my joy. Not Philip. Not anyone."

For the first time in two years, Michaela felt a true sense of deep peace surround her.

Daniel reached over and took her hand. "So what about Philip? Does he still fit into things?"

Michaela nodded her head and smiled. "I think so, but that's what I have to pray about."

❧

Michaela sat in her room later that afternoon, thinking about what she and Daniel had discussed. She knew she needed to talk to Eric, but even more important, she needed some time with her heavenly Father.

"God, I realize how much I need freedom from the past, and You're right here, waiting for me to give it up to You." Tears began to flow down her face, but she didn't attempt to wipe them away. "I need the peace You've promised. The peace that passes all understanding."

Ethen wouldn't have wanted her to sit and mope, wishing things were different. It certainly wouldn't change anything. She could almost see Ethen sitting in the chair across the room, looking at her with his smile that had been only for her.

"I have to say good-bye, Ethen," Michaela said aloud. "I have to go on with my life. I realize you would want me to be happy, and instead I've mourned for something I can never have again. I miss you so much. And Leah, with her dark hair and bright eyes. My little angel. Please take care of each other for me and know I'll never stop loving you. I just can't stop living."

It was time to move on.

≥≈

An hour later, a knock on the door jolted Michaela out of a deep slumber. In her dream, she'd been running through a green valley after someone, but in the hazy fog, she couldn't tell who it was. Pushing aside the vague impression of a tall, dark-haired farmer, she stumbled to the door and opened it a crack, still trying to wake up.

Daniel stood at the door, his hands shoved in his pockets. "I'm sorry to wake you. Hiram Williams is here to see you."

"Hiram Williams?" Michaela stifled a deep yawn.

"From church."

She shook her head, not understanding why Hiram would want to see her. "What does he want?"

Daniel grinned. "Let's just say this isn't a business call."

"Oh." Her mouth curved into a frown at the implication. "Tell him I'll be right out."

Michaela glanced in the mirror, making sure she looked presentable. She smoothed out her dress and put a stray strand of hair in place. Taking a deep breath, she went into the parlor.

"Hiram." He stood to greet her, rotating the brim of his had between his hands. "How nice to see you."

Michaela recognized the tall redhead from church. He had

a big smile and a face full of freckles. She had never spoken to him other than to say a polite hello at church services.

"I hope you don't mind me dropping by." He gave her another sheepish grin as she took a seat across from him. "I tried to catch you after church today, but you left in quite a hurry."

Michaela leaned against the back of the Boston rocker. "Daniel and I needed to get home to Emma. The baby is due in less than three weeks now."

"I'm sure they're very grateful you're here to help out with things. Running a farm is a big job. I know from experience, though winter is a bit slower." Hiram continued talking, hardly taking a breath. "I own a farm not ten miles from here. My father farmed it until he died three years ago, then I took it over. I'm an only child, so naturally, the farm is mine now."

"That's nice." Michaela forced a smile, wondering when he would get to the point of his visit.

"I had a really good crop this year." He rested his forearms against his thighs in an apparent attempt to get comfortable. Michaela smiled inwardly at the picture he made. The hefty farmer seemed out of place in a parlor filled with dainty porcelain dishes and Emma's collection of lacy sandwich plates.

"In fact, this has been the best year yet," he continued. "I won't bore you with all the details. I'm sure coming from the city, farming might not be one of your interests?"

He said it like a question, and Michaela wondered what he wanted her to say.

"Actually, I've learned a little about farming since I've been here. I have to admit, though, I'd never milked a cow before I came here."

Hiram let out a deep belly laugh. "And I've been milking

cows since the day I could walk."

Michaela gave him a weak smile and wished Daniel would come and rescue her. "Was there something you needed?"

"Well, yes, actually." Hiram cleared his throat. "Each Christmas Eve we have a big celebration. It's a wonderful time with caroling, a bonfire, and, of course, lots of food."

"Sounds like fun."

"Oh, it is. Normally we have it every year at the Hurn farm, but since he's been laid up these last few months, it will be at the Johnsons' farm. They have such a nice-sized house, and it's not as crowded."

Michaela nodded, waiting for the inevitable invitation.

"I was wondering. . .well. . .if you'd like to go with me this year."

Michaela hated to turn him down. He seemed to be a nice man, but nevertheless, she couldn't accept his invitation. "Mr. Williams. . ."

"Please, call me Hiram."

"Of course. Hiram." She started again. "I'm flattered you would want to ask me, and I'm sure I'd have a wonderful time with you. The truth is, there's someone back in Boston. We're engaged."

Hiram squirmed in his seat, then stood abruptly. "I'm sorry. I had no idea."

Michaela stood as well, feeling awkward over the entire situation. "Please understand, it's nothing personal. I'm sure there are several women at church who would love to go with you."

Hiram scratched his head, then put his hat on. "I guess I'd better get going then. I apologize for taking up your time."

"I'll see you next Sunday at church?"

"Of course. I'll be there."

Michaela followed Hiram to the door. Stepping out onto the front porch behind him, Michaela froze. Eric stood at the bottom of the steps.

"Eric?"

"Michaela." Eric turned to face her. "I stopped by to talk to you, but if you're busy. . ."

"Hiram was just leaving."

Hiram mumbled good-bye, then mounted his horse and rode off toward his farm.

"I didn't know you and Hiram were friends." Eric followed Michaela into the house.

"Actually, we're not. I mean, I don't really know him at all. He just stopped by to ask me something."

"I see."

"I noticed you weren't in church this morning." Michaela stalled for time as she sat in the chair, wondering how much Eric had heard of their conversation. Eric sat across from her, looking more nervous than Hiram had, if that were possible. "I didn't get a chance to talk to your children. Daniel wanted to hurry back to Emma."

"Ruby was sick, but she's feeling much better now."

"I'm glad to hear that."

Michaela's stomach lurched, and again she wished Daniel would come into the room, but he was in the barn and Emma was asleep.

"I came to talk to you about last night. I felt I owed you an apology, but now. . ." He stood and paced, his boots echoing across the wood floor. Turning sharply, he faced Michaela. "Why didn't you tell me you were engaged to someone in Boston?"

"I don't know." She shook her head and gazed miserably at

his clenched jaw. Why couldn't she have handled the situation better? "I owe you an apology." She bit her lower lip. "I never meant to give you the impression I was interested in you. Romantically, that is. I love being with your family, but that's it."

Michaela's heart pounded in her chest as she forced herself to continue. "When you kissed me, it took me off guard. I should have told you I'm getting married. I'm sorry."

"It certainly would have made things a lot easier if you had told me." Eric sat across from her again, his hands gripping the arms of the chair. "I assumed with all the time you were spending with the children, maybe part of it was because you enjoyed being with me as well."

"You assumed wrong." Michaela's voice rose in frustration. Immediately, she wished she could take back the harsh words, but still, it wasn't entirely her fault. She'd never meant to give him the impression she was interested in him.

"Your children are wonderful, and I've enjoyed teaching them. I've even enjoyed the few times we've talked together. But my personal life is just that—personal."

Eric sat quietly for a moment, and Michaela knew she'd hurt him.

"If you'd rather not come out to the house for any more lessons, I'd understand completely." Eric's tone sent icy shivers down her spine. "I can tell the children you're needed here with Emma."

Michaela shook her head and took a deep breath, trying to calm the pounding of her heart. "I made a commitment to the children, and I'll be there. I'll be leaving in a few weeks, anyway. I want them to get in as much practice as possible before I leave."

"The children will miss you." Eric cleared his throat and stood. "I need to get home and make sure Ruby's all right."

Michaela followed him to the door. Eric took the porch stairs two at a time and in one seamless motion jumped on his horse and rode away. She stood at the door and watched until all she could see was his shapeless form on the horizon.

twelve

"Mrs. Macintosh!" Ruby greeted her at the door of the Johnson home the night of the Christmas Eve party. Candles filled the parlor, adding warmth to the frosty night. A handful of people had already arrived and now mingled in small groups around a tree that had been decorated with mauve-colored silk bows and dainty gold balls for the occasion.

Ruby held Michaela's hand tightly, her face bright with the excitement of the holiday. "Your dress is beautiful!"

"Thank you, sweetie." Michaela glanced down at her green taffeta dress. She'd been afraid it might be a bit elaborate with its full bustle skirt and silk ribbon lace, but Emma had assured her it was perfect. Glancing at the other guests, she had to agree Emma had been right. Everyone had taken advantage of the occasion and pulled out their finest outfits.

"Tomorrow's Christmas." Ruby tugged on Michaela's arm and pulled her closer. "Do you have a present for me?"

"A present. Let me see." Michaela put her index finger against her chin and pretended to think. "I guess you'll have to wait until tomorrow to find out, but I'll let you in on a secret." Michaela bent over and whispered in Ruby's ear. "I think you'll find a little something under the tree for you from me."

Ruby in turn cupped her hands around her mouth. "Can I tell you a secret?"

"Of course." Michaela smiled, enjoying the little game with the youngster.

"I have a present for you, too."

"You do?" Michaela pretended to look surprised.

Ruby nodded and reached inside the pocket of her dark blue dress. "You said Christmas makes you sad, so I wanted to give you something to make you happy."

She held out a small gift she had obviously wrapped herself. "You don't have to wait until Christmas. You can open it right now."

"All right." Carefully, Michaela unwrapped the shiny red paper held together precariously with a white ribbon.

Ruby stood with her hands clasped behind her back, her eyes glowing with excitement.

Inside the package was a small gold-encased cameo brooch. Certainly, it had to be a family heirloom. Michaela swallowed hard, not sure what she should do. "It's beautiful, but where did you get it?"

Ruby crinkled the edge of the wrapping paper and smiled, obviously pleased with her gift. "It's mine. Pa says when we give something away that's special to us, we're giving from the heart."

Michaela glanced around the room, looking for Eric. "Your father's right, but this looks very expensive."

"What am I right about?"

Michaela drew out a sigh of relief when Eric appeared beside her. "Ruby gave me a gift for Christmas." Michaela held up the brooch, hoping Eric could read the concern in her expression.

"Where did you get this, Ruby?" Her father ran his hand across Ruby's silky hair, then pulled her gently toward him.

Ruby's chin rose as if she was determined her gift would go unchallenged. "It was Mother's, and now it's mine to give to anyone I want. I gave it to Michaela because I want her to be my new mother. I never knew my mother because God took her away to heaven, and I think it's time I had a mother like everyone else."

Michaela stood up straight, her jaw lowering in surprise.

"Ruby." Eric hesitated. "This brooch is yours to do with what you want. If you want to give it to Michaela, then that's fine. But, as much as you want a mother. . ." Eric glanced at Michaela, a note of sadness in his voice. "Michaela's going back to Boston soon. That's where she lives. She's going to marry a man there."

Ruby's smile faded, and it broke Michaela's heart to see her so disappointed. But Eric was right. She would be going home soon and could never be Ruby's mother.

"Are you sure you don't want to keep this, Ruby?" Michaela bent down, holding the gift in the palm of her hand. "I would understand if you wanted to since it was your mother's."

Ruby looked from Eric to Michaela.

"I'll tell you what, Ruby." Eric leaned over and picked up his youngest daughter. "You and I will make a special trip into town next week, just the two of us, and you can pick out a special gift for Mrs. Macintosh then. How does that sound?"

Ruby squished her lips together, contemplating her father's offer. "All right," she finally agreed. "You won't have your feelings hurt, Mrs. Macintosh?"

Michaela smiled and ran her hand down Ruby's rosy cheek. "Not at all. I'll never forget how special you made my Christmas."

Ruby grinned widely, then reached out to give Michaela a big hug, bringing her within inches of Eric's face. The back of his hand brushed Michaela's arm, and she took a step back at the brief contact.

Eric cleared his throat. "I think it's time to start the singing. Do you still feel like playing?"

Michaela nodded, thankful for the distraction.

"Wait, before you go. . ." Eric's hand touched the sleeve of her dress. Ruby had walked off and they were alone for a moment. "Can we call a truce? I'd like it if we could remain friends."

"I'd like that, too." Michaela forced a smile. "I still feel so horrible about yesterday—"

Eric held up his hand to stop her from continuing. "I'd just as soon put that behind us."

Michaela nodded and went to sit at the piano. She played song after song, and the front room rang with animated voices full of Christmas cheer. After an hour or so of singing, the festivities moved on to a contest prepared for the children. While the men got the bonfire started out behind the barn, Michaela brought out the maple syrup gingerbread cookies she had made especially for tonight, along with several colors of frosting and goodies to decorate the cookies.

The children crowded around the table in the kitchen and began to work on their cookies. Michaela was pleased at not only how seriously they took the project, but also how creative many of them were.

"This is fun." A dark-haired little boy placed two small candies on a snowman for eyes.

"Look at my star, Mrs. Macintosh." Ruby held up a cookie for her to see.

"It looks wonderful." Michaela smiled, hoping Ruby had forgiven her for not accepting her gift.

The guests mingled, both in the house and outside where

they stood near the bonfire, roasting chicken and drinking hot cocoa. It was a perfect evening.

Someone screamed outside.

Michaela hurried out onto the front porch to see what had happened. To the far left, she could see the barn. Orange and yellow flames roared with intensity, shooting up from its roof. A dozen men worked as fast as they could to put out the fire and get the animals to safety. Women huddled outside with children, keeping them away from the fire and watching in disbelief at what only minutes ago had been a time of joy and celebration.

Ruby ran after her father toward the flaming building. None of the men seemed to notice the small girl entering the burning barn. Without considering the consequences, Michaela hurried off the porch.

In a dreamlike state, Michaela ran toward the barn. All she could think of was the little girl in the fire. The flames singed the hairs on her arms, but Michaela felt nothing.

"Leah!" She screamed at the top of her lungs, desperately trying to reach her before it was too late.

"Not again, God," she cried. "Please don't let it happen again!"

Inside the barn, the heat was intense. Michaela heard a cracking sound from the ceiling.

"Leah!" Michaela screamed and ran for the little girl who stood in the path of a falling beam.

Seconds later, there was darkness. And then nothing.

thirteen

"What's going to happen to Mrs. Macintosh?" Sarah wrapped her arms around her legs, rocking back and forth on a cushioned chair. "I don't want her to die."

Eric sat with his children in the parlor, exhausted, yet unable to sleep. The barn was a total loss, though they'd managed to save most of the animals. If not for the falling snow and lack of wind, they might have lost the house as well.

The barn, though, was the least of Eric's worries. No matter what Michaela felt about him, upstairs in Rebecca's room lay the woman he loved. Michaela had saved Ruby's life and taken the brunt of the force when a beam collapsed, striking her on the back of her head.

Adam sat on the floor, resting his elbows on his knees. "Do you think Mrs. Macintosh is going to live?"

"All we can do is pray and wait for the doctor." Eric stood and walked across the room to the window. Outside, the earth was covered by a deep layer of snow.

The sun would be up in a few hours, but Christmas had been all but forgotten. Eric refused to give up hope. She had to be all right. He turned at the creaking of the stairs and the subsequent appearance of the doctor. "How is she?"

The doctor rubbed the sides of his temples with the tips of his fingers. "I honestly don't know at this point. She's asleep right now. It's difficult to know how much damage was done. There were a few burns on her arms, but thankfully they're not too serious. The wound on her head is deep, but I'm more worried about internal damage."

"What about Emma?" Daniel came in from the kitchen with a steaming cup of coffee in his hands. An hour after the fire began, his wife had gone into labor.

"It's a good thing you didn't try to take her home last night." The doctor pulled off his wire-rimmed glasses and rubbed his eyes. "The contractions are strong, but she's doing fine. It won't be long now before the baby's here. Mrs. Santon's staying with her, and I'd say in the next few hours, there'll be a new little boy or girl in the house."

Daniel let out a sigh of relief.

Setting his glasses back on the bridge of his nose, the doctor glanced around the room. "All of you need to go to bed and get some sleep. There's nothing else you can do tonight."

Eric stifled a yawn. "The doctor's right, kids. We've got a lot of work to do in the morning."

He picked up his youngest daughter, who had fallen asleep in Sarah's lap, and carried her upstairs to her room. After getting her settled, he closed the door quietly behind him, his gaze resting on the door to Rebecca's room, where Michaela lay. He cried out to God, begging Him to save her. He still loved her so much. If only she felt the same for him.

❧

The presents lay unopened under the tree Christmas morning. Slowly the children woke from a restless night and joined Eric in the parlor. Unable to sleep, he'd come downstairs in case the doctor had news for him. The fireplace cast ominous shadows on the walls as rays of morning sun crept through the window.

"Has there been any word?" Rebecca came in from the kitchen with a cup of hot coffee and handed it to her father.

"Thank you." He took a deep sip of the strong brew and shook his head. "Nothing yet."

Daniel lay sprawled across the sofa, his open gaze fixed on the ceiling. Eric doubted he'd slept, either.

There were shouts upstairs, followed by the shrill cry of a newborn.

"The baby!" Sarah jumped up from the chair she was sitting on and clapped her hands together.

Daniel bolted to the bottom of the stairs, anxiously awaiting some word about his wife and child. After a few minutes, Mrs. Santon appeared with a broad smile across her plump face. "You're a father, Daniel! Come see your son."

Daniel ran in front of her up the stairs, two at a time.

Eric drained his mug of coffee and stood, his heart aching for good news about Michaela. "There are chores to do, children. Sitting around won't help anyone. Let's all get to work. Rebecca, I'm sure the doctor and Mrs. Santon could use some breakfast, as could the rest of us."

"Certainly." Rebecca picked up his mug, then scurried into the kitchen.

Eric stretched his arms behind him, trying to relieve some of the tension. He made a mental list of what needed to be done. Not only did the charred remains of the barn need to be cleared away, but he was going to have to make plans to rebuild.

"Eric." The doctor stood at the bottom of the stairs, his clothes crumpled from staying up most of the night. "It's Michaela. She's awake now, and she's calling for you."

Eric paused. Why would she want to see him? In his mind, he was the last person Michaela would be asking for. He took a step forward. "Are you sure?"

The doctor nodded. Slowly, Eric climbed up the stairs.

He entered the room, and his heart skipped a beat when he saw her. Her eyes were open, and he could see the pain reflected in them. Several layers of gauze were wrapped around the top of her head, and one side of her face was swollen and bruised. "Hi."

She offered him a weak smile.

He sat down beside her. "How are you feeling?"

Her eyes closed briefly, then opened again. "I don't know. My head hurts and feels like it's spinning in opposite directions."

Eric pushed back a strand of hair from her face and let it tumble against the pillow. "The doctor said you wanted to see me."

A teardrop fell down her cheek. "Everything's so fuzzy. I'm scared."

He took her hand and held it tight. "Do you remember anything about last night?"

She shook her head. "I thought it was my daughter, Leah. I had to save her. I thought God was giving me another chance to bring her back." Another tear flowed down Michaela's face. "She won't ever come back, though, will she?"

Emotion welled inside Eric's chest, knowing the pain Michaela was experiencing was not only physical. "It was Ruby in the fire, Michaela. You saved her life."

Her free hand touched the side of her temple. "It hurts so bad."

Eric wished he could take away her pain. Wished he could erase the scars from the past that had been ripped open last night. Hoping a distraction would help, he told her about Emma's baby.

Michaela smiled at the news. "What did they finally decide to name him?"

"Nathaniel James."

"I like that." She shifted in the bed but made no effort to pull away from his grasp.

She closed her eyes, and he wondered if she'd drifted off to sleep. Deciding to slip out and let her rest, he pulled his hand free and stood to leave the room.

"Please don't leave me." Her eyes were wide open now, and the glazed look he'd noticed before was gone.

"I'm so sorry this had to happen." He longed to hold her in his arms, but instead he sat down beside her and took her hand again. "I know it reminds you of what happened to your husband and daughter."

She nodded and squeezed his hand.

There was something he had to tell her. "I won't say this again, but when I saw that beam fall on you. . ." He closed his eyes, and for a moment he was there again, seeing the horror in her eyes, the screams that filled the air, the panic within his chest. "I knew without a doubt I loved you and didn't want to lose you."

He raked his free hand through his hair. He shouldn't be telling her this. Not here, not this way. She was in love with someone else. But she had asked for him. . .

"I know there's someone else, but I just need you to know how I feel."

Her voice was quiet, barely above a whisper. "I don't know how I feel anymore. If I love him, then why do I want you with me right now? Please stay with me." She held tight to his hand.

Eric wondered if she knew what she was saying.

The doctor stepped into the room to check on her. "She needs to rest."

Eric turned back to Michaela, who had fallen asleep. A

peaceful look covered her face, and he resisted the urge to run his finger across her cheek.

"After a couple of days, she should be all right. The beam must have skimmed her head instead of actually hitting her directly. That's probably what saved her life."

"She saved my little girl's life as well."

ঌ

Three days later, the doctor allowed Michaela and Emma to go home. The cleanup for the barn was almost finished, and Eric thanked God the snow had stopped any further damage, especially to the house. Two chickens had died, but the livestock had survived and was now holed up in Daniel's barn until another shelter could be built.

The morning after Michaela went home, Eric saddled up his horse and headed for Daniel's farm, needing to see for himself how she was doing.

"Good morning, Eric," Daniel called out from the front porch.

"Guess you have your hands full." Eric dismounted the horse and pulled his coat closer around him to block the chilly wind that had picked up.

Daniel finished hammering a loose porch rail, then greeted Eric with a firm handshake. "Several of the women at church have already been by with meals and have even helped clean the house for me."

Eric held up the pouch he was carrying. "Rebecca sent over some homemade bread and jam with me."

"No one's going hungry around here!"

"How is the baby?" Eric followed Daniel inside the house, thankful for the warmth from the stone fireplace.

"Besides the fact he keeps us up all night?" Daniel let out a deep chuckle. "Couldn't be better. He's perfect."

"I remember those nighttime feedings." Eric set the gift on a side table. "How's Michaela?"

"I think she's asleep. The doctor says she'll recover fine as long as she gets enough rest."

"The kids have been begging to come see her, but I told them they needed to wait until she's up and around." Eric stood in front of the crackling flames and rubbed his icy hands together.

"Maybe tomorrow. Would you like me to see if she's awake?" Daniel asked as a hungry cry from the baby sounded from the bedroom.

Eric nodded. "If you don't mind."

A minute later, Daniel came out of Michaela's room.

"I'm sorry, Eric." He shut the door behind him. "She's sound asleep. This whole ordeal has been both emotionally and physically draining for her."

"I know." He tried not to worry, but he knew the experience had been traumatic for her. And he wanted to be with her. "Please tell her I came by and if she needs anything, I'm here. Anything at all."

"I'll tell her."

❧

Michaela groaned and pulled out the last dozen stitches of the sweater she was knitting for the new baby. "Remind me not to attempt another project like this."

Emma chuckled as Michaela held up the lopsided sweater. "Nathaniel won't care. I'm just glad you're up and around." Emma picked up a skein of blue yarn and laid it in her lap.

"I feel so much better."

"He's such a good little boy." Emma watched her son sleep in the small crib beside her in the parlor. "I can't believe how small he is."

Daniel walked in from the kitchen with a slice of cake Mrs. Winters had sent over. The grin that crossed his lips hadn't left his face since the baby's arrival. He sat down on the sofa beside his wife. "Eric came by earlier, Michaela, but you were asleep. He asked if he could bring his children by to see you tomorrow if the weather is not too bad. They've been worried about you."

Michaela sighed. She could remember every word of her last conversation with Eric. She'd asked him to stay. For some reason, she'd needed him beside her to take away the fear she felt.

He'd told her he loved her.

She choked back the wave of emotion, confused by her reaction. If she wasn't careful, she'd start crying again.

"I'm sorry." She set the sweater down and walked over to the fireplace. Flames crackled. She could smell the soot and feel the intensity of the blaze. "I haven't felt like myself lately."

"It's all right." Emma's voice was reassuring.

"When I saw Ruby running toward the barn and the fire, I relived it all over again. It was Leah, and God was giving me a second chance to save her." She turned around to face them. "I know it sounds crazy."

Emma shook her head. "It's not crazy at all."

The wind howled and the windows shook with the impact.

"There's another storm coming." Daniel stood up and looked out the window. "I'd better go out to the barn and make sure the animals are secure. It's likely to be a bad one."

"Bundle up," Emma insisted. "The temperature has dropped."

Michaela shivered unconsciously, wishing she could get Eric and the feel of his strong hand around hers out of her mind.

fourteen

Philip Macintosh got off the train and stood on the tiny platform, wondering what his next move should be. Snow flurries whipped around him beneath a darkened sky. Maybe he had been foolish for coming to Cranton without telling anyone, but after receiving the telegram from Daniel about Michaela's accident, he'd had no choice.

Philip tightened his long coat against the wind. He couldn't believe how desolate the town looked. The snow had drifted into deep piles along the sides of the buildings, and few people braved the harsh elements. He didn't blame them.

The sun would be setting soon, taking with it any lingering traces of light. His best option would be to find the nearest hotel and get a good night's sleep before traveling to Daniel's farm in the morning.

Philip picked up his bag and started for the center of town. The hotel proved easy to find, and soon he made his way through the front door, thankful for the warmth of the lobby. Rubbing his hands together, he took a seat at a table next to the fireplace and ordered a cup of hot coffee.

A man was talking to the hotel manager at the nearby desk. Philip turned his head when he heard mention of Michaela's brother.

"I hear Daniel's wife had a boy." The manager leaned his elbows on the counter.

The second man nodded. "I saw him yesterday. They

seem to be doing great."

"Sorry to hear about the fire that destroyed your barn," the first man continued.

"I'm just thankful no one was killed."

Philip leaned toward the men. What about Michaela?

"So Daniel's sister, Michaela. Is she all right?" The manager slid his glasses up the bridge of his nose.

"Got quite a knot on her head, but she's doing fine. We were worried for a while, but the doctor says with a little rest, there shouldn't be any complications."

"That's good to hear."

"I need to get on home, George. I'm afraid it'll be a rough ride. I wouldn't have come in today if it hadn't been absolutely necessary. Been the first break in the weather all week, and now things are stirring up again. I've got to get home before dark, and at that I'm not likely to make it."

The man headed toward the door with broad, determined steps. Philip decided this was his chance.

"Excuse me, sir." Philip stood and quickly crossed the room and introduced himself. "My name's Philip Macintosh, Michaela Macintosh's brother-in-law. I just got into town, and I wondered if you could tell me how to get to her brother's farm. I guess I'll have to wait until morning, though."

"Do you have a horse?"

"No, sir, I just got off the train."

"I'm on my way home right now, and my farm is right past theirs. I had to pick up a few supplies, so I brought the sled. You can come with me if you'd like." The man shook Philip's hand. "Name's Eric Johnson, by the way. We'd better get going if we're going to make it before nightfall."

"Nice to meet you. I sure appreciate this." Philip left enough money for the coffee and a tip and followed Eric out the door. "Didn't think I could make it out there tonight."

"God must have wanted our paths to cross. I had planned to leave over an hour ago, but I got held up." Eric raised his voice against the howling wind as they hurried to the sled. "Another storm isn't far behind us. I guess you heard about the accident."

"That's why I'm here."

"She's doing fine now. The doctor said the beam that hit her just missed doing some very serious damage."

"I'm just thankful she's alive."

The snow was picking up and the wind whipped against Philip, making further conversation impossible. He climbed into the sled, anxious for the moment he'd see Michaela again.

&

"Looks like another severe storm's about to hit." Michaela paced the living room floor, wishing the long stretch of winter weather would be over soon. For the past week, the storms had come one after another, and as soon as one let up, there seemed to be another one hitting even harder. She knew that Eric had planned to go into town today, and she prayed he'd made it home safely.

"You're pacing again," Emma commented as Michaela started across the room once again.

Michaela shrugged and continued her trek. "The storm's getting worse."

Emma stuck her needle into the taut fabric, then pulled it out gently. "Would you like to help me with the quilt? It would help you get your mind off whatever is bothering you."

"Eric was supposed to go into town. I was hoping he made it

home all right. I'd hate for the children to be alone right now."

She looked at the quilt Emma patiently stitched together, piece by piece. The vivid reds, greens, and yellows were already starting to form the intricate pattern. If only life was as simple as following a pattern. Instead, it was full of detours, turns, and at times, heartache.

Someone pounded on the front door. Michaela jumped. "Who could that be?"

Daniel opened the door.

"Eric!" Relief flooded through her as she hurried toward the door. She stopped when she noticed a man standing next to him, bundled in a heavy coat. "Philip?"

"Boy, are you a sight for sore eyes." Philip picked her up and swung her around. "I didn't think I'd ever get here."

"How did you. . . ?" Michaela looked to Eric, then back to Philip, confused.

Eric strode across the room to the crackling fire. "Found your brother-in-law in town as I was leaving. Didn't want him to have to spend the night in town."

Philip held her for a moment, then went to stand by the fireplace beside Eric, his gaze never leaving Michaela's face.

"After I got the telegram about the accident, I left Boston on the next train." Philip rubbed his hands together. "Never imagined it would be so cold." He turned to Eric. "I'm sure Michaela's told you. We're planning to get married as soon as she gets back to Boston."

Eric's gaze locked momentarily with Michaela's. She looked away, not able to bear the mark of pain in his eyes. What had she done?

Eric shuffled his feet and cleared his throat. "I need to get home before this storm blows full force." His voice was void of emotion as he quickly made his escape to the front door. "It was nice to meet you, Mr. Macintosh."

A brief gust of wind blew in, and he was gone.

Michaela's gaze lingered on the closed door for a moment before she turned back to Philip. "I can't believe you're here."

He smiled at her and took her hands in his. "I was so worried. I know it's crazy to come all the way out here, but I just had to see for myself that you were all right."

"I'm fine." Michaela squeezed his hands, then showed him where the board had hit her. "Just a very bad bump on the head and a headache that lasted for days."

Emma stood up and motioned Daniel to follow her into the kitchen so the two of them could be alone. "We'll get you some hot tea."

"Michaela." Once they'd left the room, Philip ran his thumb down the side of her cheek, his face lit with relief. "You don't know how much I've missed you."

He reached down and kissed her slowly on the lips. Michaela pushed away any feelings of doubt. Seeing him put everything back into perspective. She was going to marry Philip, and together they'd adopt Anna.

fifteen

"There you are." Michaela stopped along the side of the Johnsons' new barn, where Philip stood high up on a ladder, nailing shingles onto the roof. The last couple of days had been a whirlwind of activity as the men in the community gathered to rebuild Eric's barn.

Philip finished driving a nail before glancing down at Michaela. He blew out a puff of air and smiled. "Hi."

Michaela took a step back and studied the gabled structure, amazed at how much work had been accomplished. "You men have done a wonderful job on Eric's new barn."

"Good thing there was a break in the weather." Philip looped his hammer on his belt and climbed down before stretching his back. "Is that for me?"

Michaela handed Philip the steaming mug of coffee. He took a deep sip. "I sure needed this. The snow might have stopped, but it's still icy cold."

She shoved her hands into the deep pockets of her wool coat. "Lunch will be ready soon. There's quite a feast prepared, including roast beef, ham, potatoes, bread—"

"Stop, you're making my stomach growl." Philip held up one of his hands and grinned. "I want to finish the section I'm working on, then I'll come in."

He took another sip, keeping his eyes focused on her. She could feel the heat rising in her cheeks at his intense gaze.

She tilted her head, lowering her brows in question. "What is it?"

"The trip out here's been good for you, hasn't it?"

Michaela nodded and breathed in deeply. There was a peace about her she hadn't felt for a long time. "I've been able to sort through things—let go of some things from the past."

Philip took a final gulp of the coffee and handed the empty cup back to Michaela. "There's a glow about you that you didn't have back home. I'm glad to see you happy and relaxed. We've all been worried about you."

"And who is we?" Michaela chuckled and fingered the rim of the mug. It was nice to have someone fuss over her.

The blue of his eyes lightened in the bright sunlight. "Me, for one. Aunt Clara. Caroline."

"You've talked a lot about Caroline this week."

He smiled at her teasing. "She and I tried to visit Anna as often as we could. Anna enjoyed it."

"I'm glad."

He ran his gloved hand down her sleeve. "The board said we could adopt Anna as soon as we're married."

Her heart soared at the possibility that the three of them could be a family. "I can't wait to see her."

Philip pulled the hammer out of his belt and jingled the sack of nails he held. "I'd better get finished. Can't believe we're heading home tomorrow. Seems like I just got off that train, and now I have to get right back on."

❧

Philip paused to watch as Michaela turned around and walked back toward the house. Tomorrow they'd leave for Boston, and in a few weeks she'd become his wife. Eric approached Michaela, halfway between Philip and the house. She pushed a stray piece of hair behind one ear and fiddled with the mug.

"The barn looks wonderful."

Michaela raised her head and smiled at Eric. They were close enough that Philip could hear their conversation.

"I'm grateful for all the help I've got."

"Eric, I. . ."

A loud ring sounded from the porch as someone hit the dinner bell.

Clang.

Clang.

"I wanted to tell you. . ."

Clang.

Clang.

"Come on, let's eat." Someone slapped Eric on the back as three of the men who had been working on the barn surrounded him. "I'm starved as a bear."

Philip watched as Michaela stood still in the snow while the men joked and laughed on their way to get their lunch. Her lips formed a frown, but he couldn't read her expression. What had she wanted to say to Eric?

Philip decided to join the group for lunch and finish the shingles later. He hurried across the hard ground to catch up to where Michaela still stood. "Ready to eat?"

"Yes." He watched as she glanced one last time at Eric before turning back to him. "Yes. I'm ready."

Philip cupped Michaela's elbow with his hand, but his focus remained on the man ahead of them. Was Eric the one who had brought life back to Michaela's heart?

❧

"I can't believe you're leaving." Emma cleared the last cup from the breakfast table, then wiped it down with a wet cloth.

Michaela held the sleeping baby in her arms, enjoying his sweet fragrance. "I'll be back. I have to make sure little Nate knows who his favorite aunt is."

"The wagon's ready." Daniel opened the back door and came into the kitchen.

Michaela handed the baby back to Emma, trying not to cry. She wrapped her arms around her sister-in-law for a moment. "I'm going to miss you so much."

"We're going to miss you, too."

"I want you both to know how much I've appreciated your hospitality these past few days," Philip said as he picked up the last bag and held open the front door for Michaela. "I know it was a bit unexpected."

"Just promise to take good care of her." Emma reached up and kissed him on the cheek.

"You know I will."

Michaela hurried toward the wagon, struggling to hold back the tears.

She had said good-bye to the Johnson children the night before. There had been a few tears shed, even by the boys, and Michaela promised she would write as soon as she got to Boston. There had been no time alone with Eric. No time to tell him how sorry she was for everything. She let Philip help her into the wagon, forcing herself to put Eric out of her mind.

The ride to town seemed short, and Michaela wondered if she'd have a chance to come back again. She looked out across the snow-covered ground. A bird flew overhead, singing a lonely tune. Crystals of ice sparkled in the snow below. She studied the scene, trying to memorize each detail so as not to forget.

At the station, Michaela stood silently on the platform as Philip put her bags on the train.

"I'm going to miss you, Michaela." Daniel wrapped his arms around her tightly. "Promise you'll come back."

Michaela smiled through the tears, trying desperately to hold on to her emotions. She would miss them all so much.

"All aboard!"

"It's time, Michaela."

Taking one last look at her brother, Michaela followed Philip onto the train and waved good-bye for the final time.

❧

He'd been a fool.

Eric pushed his stallion as fast as he could across the frozen terrain. Forests of pine trees seemed to fly by, but only one thing seemed clear at the moment. Michaela. He never should have let her leave without talking to her. He'd let his pride get in the way of letting himself become vulnerable.

At the Cranton station, he jumped off the horse and quickly tied the lead rope to a post. His stomach turned as he caught sight of the empty platform. He was too late.

❧

Michaela sat across from Philip and looked out the window of the train, waiting for it to leave the small station. The familiar valley stretched out before her, a sharp contrast from the bustling streets of Boston.

"You'd better hurry if you're going to get off the train."

Michaela turned to Philip, lowering her brow in question. "What did you say?"

He leaned forward and took her hands. "From the moment I arrived, I saw something in your eyes when you looked at him. You've never looked at me that way."

Michaela opened her mouth to respond, but he put a finger to her lips. "I've been awake all night trying to decide what to do. I'm a part of what's familiar to you, what's comfortable. . . . But you don't love me, Michaela. You love Eric. And if I'm not mistaken, he loves you as well."

Michaela closed her eyes, trying to make sense of everything. Philip had been a part of her life for so long. At a time when she'd needed him, he'd always been there. Yes, he was familiar and comfortable. . .but was that all? "I don't know. I. . ."

"Do you love him?"

She closed her eyes and could see Eric—the dimple on his right cheek when he smiled. The sound of his laugh. The tenderness he showed to his children. She loved him. "I didn't want to."

"I know." Philip reached out and wiped away a tear that had fallen down her cheek. "Go on. You'd better hurry."

❧

Michaela stepped off the train moments before it roared away from the station. It was clear to her now. In not wanting to let go of the past, she'd held tight to what was familiar and comfortable. And in turn, she'd confused feelings of safety and protection for love. Her relationship with Philip would always be important, but she knew now she could never love him.

White light reflected off the snow that still covered parts of the ground. She watched the train pull out of the station, slowly picking up speed until she could see only a small puff of smoke lingering on the horizon.

Stepping out of the shadow of the station building, she saw Eric cross the street toward her.

"Eric."

"Michaela?" His surprise to see her was obvious.

"You came to see me off?" She didn't know what to say now that he stood in front of her.

"I wanted to, but I thought you were leaving with Philip. Why are you still here?"

Tears streamed down her cheeks. Eric took a step closer and gently wiped them away with his hand.

"I realized I love you." Michaela's voice was barely above a whisper. "And I couldn't go with Philip. I thought I could love him, but then I met you and everything changed. I've just been too stubborn to admit it, even to myself."

A smile spread across Eric's face. "Did you say you love me?"

Michaela nodded shyly, surprised at her boldness.

Eric let out a shout of joy. "So you'll marry me?"

A burst of laugher exploded from her lips. "You're asking me if I'll marry you?"

"Will you?"

There were no longer any doubts as to who she wanted to spend the rest of her life with. "Yes!"

He picked her up by her waist, swung her around, and gently put her back down. He brought her face toward his and kissed her slowly. Michaela laid her hands against his chest, enjoying the sweet taste of his lips against hers.

After a moment, he pulled back, still cupping her face in his hands. "I suppose this isn't the most appropriate place for displays of affection, but I can't help it. I love you, Michaela Macintosh."

Michaela just looked at him, realizing she'd been given a second chance for love. "What will the kids think?"

"They're going to be six of the happiest kids in the county. I've seen nothing but gloomy faces around my place since you told them you were leaving."

Eric brushed back the tears from her cheeks with the back of his hand. "I was going to buy a train ticket for Boston and come after you. You must be some catch to have men traipsing all over the country for you."

"I finally realized the truth. There's only one man for me."

No more words were needed as Michaela felt his strong arms surround her and his lips met hers.

epilogue

Six months later

Michaela paced the wooden platform for what seemed to be the hundredth time as she watched for the twelve o'clock train to arrive from Boston.

"It's late." She turned to her husband, who stood beside her with a broad grin on his face.

"I don't think you were this nervous on our wedding day," Eric teased.

Michaela smoothed out her plum-colored dress and adjusted the straw hat that shaded her face from the hot summer sun.

"I just want everything to be perfect." She stopped and stood still for the first time in minutes.

A whistle sounded in the distance, and Michaela looked out across the green valley to see the long-awaited train.

"Kids," Eric called out, "the train will be here any moment."

The six Johnson children hurried over to where Eric and Michaela stood, just in time for the steam engine to make its appearance in town.

"Do you think she'll like me?" Ruby pulled on the collar of her dress in an attempt to straighten it.

"She's going to love you," Michaela assured her with a smile as she tugged playfully on one of Ruby's pigtails.

Brakes screeched and the train came to a stop in front of them.

"Aunt Clara!" Michaela ran toward her aunt as soon as she disembarked from the train.

"You don't know how good it is to see you, child," her aunt said, looking deep into Michaela's eyes.

"You look wonderful, Aunt Clara." Michaela squeezed her tight again. "I don't know if it's your new dress or marriage, but I will have to assume it's the marriage."

Aunt Clara laughed as Ben White, her husband of two months, followed her onto the platform. "Then it's done wonders for you as well. It does seem there's been a rash of weddings lately."

Michaela looked up to see Philip come off the train followed by his new bride, Caroline, looking radiant in her bright yellow dress.

The three friends hugged, amazed at how much had changed in such a short time.

Michaela's eyes searched the doorway of the train.

"Don't forget about me." Michaela's heart melted as she looked up at the sound of Anna's voice.

"I prayed this day would come." Michaela felt her heart was about to burst. As Anna stepped onto the platform, Michaela knelt down and scooped the little girl into her arms.

"I love you, Anna," she said.

"And I love you, Mama."

"I can't believe my entire family is here." Michaela wiped a tear from the corner of her eye, still holding Anna tight. "I don't ever remember feeling so happy, so complete."

"God does have marvelous ways of working things together for the good of His children, doesn't He?" Eric took his place behind her and wrapped his strong arms firmly around her waist.

"Aunt Clara is happily married to Ben." Happiness radiated in Michaela's voice. "Philip realized he loved Caroline. But best of all is Anna. I have to thank God every day that couple decided to adopt only a little boy. I never imagined it would end this way."

Eric turned Michaela to face him.

"It's not the end, Michaela," he said and kissed her gently on the lips. "It's only the beginning."

A Letter To Our Readers

Dear Reader:

In order that we might better contribute to your reading enjoyment, we would appreciate your taking a few minutes to respond to the following questions. We welcome your comments and read each form and letter we receive. When completed, please return to the following:

Fiction Editor
Heartsong Presents
PO Box 719
Uhrichsville, Ohio 44683

1. Did you enjoy reading *Michaela's Choice* by Lisa Harris?
   ❏ Very much! I would like to see more books by this author!
   ❏ Moderately. I would have enjoyed it more if

   _____
   _____
   _____

2. Are you a member of **Heartsong Presents**?   ❏ Yes   ❏ No
   If no, where did you purchase this book? _____
   _____

3. How would you rate, on a scale from 1 (poor) to 5 (superior), the cover design? _____

4. On a scale from 1 (poor) to 10 (superior), please rate the following elements.

   ____ Heroine   ____ Plot
   ____ Hero   ____ Inspirational theme
   ____ Setting   ____ Secondary characters

5. These characters were special because?_____

_____

_____

6. How has this book inspired your life?_____

_____

_____

7. What settings would you like to see covered in future
   Heartsong Presents books? _____

_____

_____

8. What are some inspirational themes you would like to see
   treated in future books? _____

_____

_____

9. Would you be interested in reading other **Heartsong
   Presents** titles? ❏ Yes ❏ No

10. Please check your age range:
   ❏ Under 18   ❏ 18-24
   ❏ 25-34   ❏ 35-45
   ❏ 46-55   ❏ Over 55

Name_____

Occupation _____

Address _____

City_____ State_____ Zip_____

Heartsong

Presents

$\mathcal{H}$EARTSONG ♥ PRESENTS
Love Stories
Are Rated G!

That's for godly, gratifying, and of course, great! If you love a thrilling love story but don't appreciate the sordidness of some popular paperback romances, **Heartsong Presents** is for you. In fact, **Heartsong Presents** is the premiere inspirational romance book club featuring love stories where Christian faith is the primary ingredient in a marriage relationship.

Sign up today to receive your first set of four, never-before-published Christian romances. Send no money now; you will receive a bill with the first shipment. You may cancel at any time without obligation, and if you aren't completely satisfied with any selection, you may return the books for an immediate refund!

Imagine. . .four new romances every four weeks—two historical, two contemporary—with men and women like you who long to meet the one God has chosen as the love of their lives. . .all for the low price of $10.99 postpaid.

To join, simply complete the coupon below and mail to the address provided. **Heartsong Presents** romances are rated G for another reason: They'll arrive Godspeed!

YES! Sign me up for Hearts♥ng!

NEW MEMBERSHIPS WILL BE SHIPPED IMMEDIATELY!
Send no money now. We'll bill you only $10.99 post-paid with your first shipment of four books. Or for faster action, call toll free 1-800-847-8270.

NAME _____

ADDRESS _____

CITY_____STATE_____ ZIP_____

MAIL TO: HEARTSONG PRESENTS, P.O. Box 721, Uhrichsville, Ohio 44683
or visit www.heartsongpresents.com